CAMERON 2

Jade Jones

Interact with the Author:

Add me on Facebook: Author Jade Jones

Follow me on Twitter: Jade_Jones89

Blogger: http://authorjadejones.blogspot.com/

This novel is a work of fiction. Any reference to real people, events, establishments, or locales are intended only to give the fiction a sense of reality or authenticity. Other names, characters, and incidents occurring in the work are either the product of the author's imagination or are used fictitiously, as are those fictionalized events and incidents that involve real persons. Any character that happens to share the name of a person who is any acquaintance of the author, past or present, is purely coincidental and is in no way intended to be an actual account involving that person.

Acknowledgments

First I would like to thank the Lord for blessing me with the gift of creativity and also helping me to perfect it. I would also like to thank my mentor/fellow author/friend, Chyna Dahl. You've helped me improve my craft and taught me so much and for that I will be forever grateful. Thank you to my test readers, and a special thanks to all the fellow authors who've contributed to me perfecting my craft. To all my readers and supporters, thank you.

Chapter 1

Jude slowly pulled me close to him. “I know you’re a big girl, Cameron,” he said. “I know you’re capable of takin’ care of yourself. I been got that vibe from you when you declined me payin’ for your school.” He kissed my cheek. “But bay, it’s okay to let someone else take the load off you. I told you, I ain’t like the last nigga.”

He tilted my chin upwards and placed a soft kiss on my lips. “I love you,” he admitted.

It was crazy how I had gone through so much shit over the last couple months. X-Rated dying, finding out about Poca and Silk, and then Poca ending up getting killed. I had suffered pain and losses but at least one good thing came out of it all.

“I love you too,” I told him.

Jude took my hands in his and stared into my eyes. “So, I’m gonna ask you again…” A smile played in the corner of his lips. “Are you feelin’ the condo?” he asked. “Do you like it?”

I twisted my mouth up for good measure. “It’s aight,” I said sarcastically.

He chuckled. “Oh, it’s just aight, huh?”

“Yep. It’s aight,” I laughed.

Jude pulled me closer to him and kissed me once more.

***

The following week, I moved all my belongings into me and Jude’s new condo, with some assistance from his brother

Jerrell and his cousin, Tez. Truthfully, I was a little hesitant about relocating. I had been living in the Cleveland State dorms for the past two years and although it wasn't some luxurious loft in downtown Cleveland, I had grown accustomed to calling it home. Besides that, I had never even lived with a man.

Silk had been asking me for months to move in with him and I denied his request each and every time. At the moment, I was deeply in love with him but I wasn't sure that I wanted to move in with him just yet. However, with Jude it was different. He was different. He was protective—but not in a domineering way like Silk had been. Silk was just plain old possessive. Jude was a lot more respectful, and he was overall a good man to me.

Staring lovingly at Jude as he drove us home, I couldn't help but think how blessed I was to have him in my life. Every day he somehow managed to garner a little bit more of my love and respect for him.

Jude turned the volume down to the Self Made 2 CD we were listening to. "That spot was nice," he said. "We gon' have to go there again sometime soon," he told me.

We had just come from Shooters on the Water—a classy restaurant located in the Flatts in downtown Cleveland. It was both of our first time going to the restaurant, which was also located on the lake, and I absolutely enjoyed myself. I loved being able to be on the water and drink and dance all at the same time. The great food was also a plus.

"Yeah we can do that," I agreed.

"We been so busy gettin' settled in and shit…I ain't get a chance to handle this in a while," Jude suddenly said before giving my bare thigh a squeeze.

Tonight I had decided to wear a chain print bandeau playsuit with a pair of tangerine platform pumps. Always a fashionista, I strived to look glamorous whenever I stepped out—especially while on the arm of my man.

Jude was absolutely right in what he had said. We had only been living in the Clifton Pointe condominiums for a week and things had been a tad bit hectic getting settled in. Especially for Jude who had just relocated back to his hometown from Columbus, Ohio. Between settling in and running the new car dealership he and his brother, Jerrell had just opened up, we had not had much time to indulge in our own sexual pleasures. Tonight was actually our first outing since we had officially moved in together.

"So when you gon' handle it?" I teased.

Jude looked over at me and smiled mischievously before focusing his attention back on the road. "Girl you gon' make me pull this whip over teasin' me like that," he said.

I paid his playful warning no mind as I decided to take the initiative. We had just crossed the Superior-Ontario Bridge when I unfastened my seat belt and leaned over in my seat.

Jude chuckled. "What you doing, bay?"

I ignored his question as I proceeded to unbutton his Levis Jeans. Normally, I was never this spontaneous when it came to sex but right now I was feeling like trying something new and fun with my man.

After unzipping his jeans, I pulled his rigid dick through the opening of his boxers.

"Damn, Cameron," he groaned as I took him in my mouth right there in the car. It felt good to be impetuous for a change and I could tell he was enjoying the spontaneity of it all.

Jude placed one hand on the nape of my neck as my head bobbed up and down his length. "Damn, bay. Your ass gon' make me crash," he laughed.

I quickly lifted my head from his lap. "Pull over," I suggested. I couldn't wait anymore. I wanted him that damn bad.

Jude continued to drive down West 25th street until he located a dark and quiet side street. Pulling his car alongside the curb, he killed the engine but left the music on. Wale and Omarion's "This Thing of Ours" played through the speakers of the Audi truck—that Jude had brought for me a couple months ago.

I sat up in my seat and hurriedly pulled my pink thong off. Jude pulled his jeans down low enough to get it in before reclining his seat. Without deliberation, I climbed over the seat and straddled him.

"Mmm," I moaned as I slid down on his pole.

He thrust his hips forward in order to get his full length inside me.

"Shit," he cursed as I gently bounced up and down. He took hold of my hips as I rode him like a horse jockey.

"Damn. It's so wet, bay," he said. "You finna make me cum fast," he warned me.

"Not yet, ba—" Before I could get the sentence out I felt an unmistakable hot liquid shoot inside me.

I stared down at Jude in disdain.

"My fault babe." His cheeks quickly flushed indicating he was a tad bit embarrassed by his unexpected premature orgasm.

I slowly climbed off top of him and plopped back down in my seat with a pouty kid face and all. This was the first time I had yet to get mine. Usually we always wore protection whenever we made love but we were both so caught up in the lustful moment that a condom was the last thing on either one of our minds.

He reached over and softly pinched my left cheek. "Don't worry, baby. I got you when we get back to the crib."

My lips formed into a slight smirk as I crossed my arms over my petite breasts. "Yeah, you'd better," I smiled.

He pulled his jeans up and buttoned them. "You got that, babe. I'ma put in work too."

I laughed. "You hollin'!"

"Naw, for real—"

The sudden sound of sirens blaring behind us quickly interrupted him.

"Fuck," Jude cursed under his breath as he stared into the rearview mirror at the flashing sirens. "Ain't this about a bitch?" He quickly sat up in his seat and ironed his clothes with his hands.

I quickly did the same. "Relax, babe," I told him.

The lone officer stepped out of his squad car at the same time Jude turned the music off. At the most, we probably looked suspicious but I knew we hadn't done anything wrong so I wasn't all that worried. Besides, our clothes were on so they couldn't pin us with indecent exposure.

Jude stared into the side view mirror as the cop slowly approached the driver's side. He hesitantly lowered the window. "Can I help you officer?" he asked.

"What are you kids doing over in the cut like this?" the officer asked in a stern tone.

"Well, we were um actually…um…"

The cop quickly cut Jude off. "Let me see your license, young man."

As Jude quickly fetched his wallet, I noticed the officer take a small whiff of his surroundings as if trying to detect a hint of marijuana.

Jude handed the officer his identification card.

I started to explain to the cop that the truck was in my name anyway but he quickly walked off to run Jude's license number. I eased back in my seat and patiently waited for this all to be over.

Jude tapped his thumbs on the steering wheel. "Really, though? They be on some straight trash. I swear they do."

"Yeah, I know," I agreed. "But let's just stay cool. Don't give him any reason to fuck with us anymore than he already is."

"Yeah .You right, bay," he agreed.

We waited in the truck for several minutes before the officer finally returned wearing a disapproving expression on his face. My heart sank into the pit of my stomach. Suddenly, I didn't feel so self-assured that everything was okay. Especially when a second squad car pulled behind the officer's.

What the hell is going on, I thought.

"Sir, I'm gonna have to ask you to step out the vehicle," the officer said.

"Is there a problem?" Jude asked.

My heart rate sped up once it was confirmed that something was obviously wrong. "What's going on?" I spoke up.

"Sir, just step out the car," the officer repeated in a stern tone.

Jude looked over at me with a concerned expression before hesitantly opening up his door. The minute he climbed out the truck, the officer grabbed his left forearm and twisted it behind his back. Slamming him against the side of the truck, it was evident that Jude was being placed under arrest.

Without deliberation, I quickly jumped out and rounded the truck. "What's going on?!" I yelled.

Suddenly, the second officer approached us, holding his arm out in front of me so that I could not get past him. “Ma’am, I am gonna have to ask you to step back,” he said.

“Step back?! I wanna know why ya’ll arrestin’ my boyfriend!” I yelled.

The officer held me back while Jude was being read his Miranda rights. He was also informed that a warrant had been issued for his immediate arrest. Evidently, this shit was a surprise to the both of us.

“Cameron, its gon’ be alright. Get in contact with my brother—” Jude’s sentence was cut short after the handcuffs were clasped onto his wrist. “Aye, man can you loosen this shit?!”

The smart ass officer ignored Jude’s request and instead of unloosening the handcuffs, he snatched him up and shoved him towards the nearest squad car.

“*What the fuck is going on*?!” I screamed.

The officer gave me a gentle shove, silently warning me not to come any closer.

“Cam, do what I said!” Jude hollered before he was forced into the back of the squad car.

Chapter 2

I dialed Jerrell's cell phone number the minute I hopped into the driver seat. Oddly enough, I was sent straight to voicemail. I assumed his cell phone had to be either off or the battery had died. I hadn't seen or spoken to Jerrell since he had helped us move into our home a week ago.

After wiping my tears away, I prepared for the short drive back home. So many thoughts were running through my mind on the account of what had just happened. This night had gone from being a romantic evening to a damn unexpected disaster.

Fifteen minutes later, I pulled the truck into my designated parking spot and climbed out. Pulling my phone out my purse, I decided to try Jerrell's number once more—however, the sudden sound of footsteps behind me caused me to drop my cell phone. Understandably, my nerves were on edge since the incident that had just taken place.

Subconsciously, I knelt down to pick my cell phone up—an arm suddenly reached out before I could and beat me at the task of retrieving it. The minute I looked up, my gaze was met with a pair of cold, dark eyes.

"What the fuck are you doing you here?" I asked in a low tone. Anger and fear coursed through my veins as I stared into the eyes of a person that had caused me more than enough unbearable pain.

Silk slowly stood up with my Sony Xperia clutched tightly within his palm. A slight smirk tugged at his full lips as he stared at me.

How the hell did he know where I lived, I thought.

When it came to Silk, I usually had no idea what his intentions were and I damn sure didn't trust whatever he had in mind. He didn't even look like himself as he stood before me. The clean cut, handsome man that I was once used to now appeared stressed out and weary. Dark bags resided underneath his eyes and they had a strange look to them. They say the eyes communicate feelings words cannot.

Silk took a step closer to me and I took a few steps back. It seemed like only yesterday I could remember him storming into my dorm room and assaulting me viciously. That nightmare was painted vividly in my head and I doubted I would forget it any time soon.

"You actin' surprised to see me," he said. "Shit, we *did* used to have somethin' special?" He smiled. "Or did you forget?"

It was apparent that Silk would not leave the past in the past. For reasons beyond me understanding, he just couldn't move the hell on.

"I didn't forget. But you must've forgotten about that restraining order," I reminded him. "No more than one hundred yards. Remember?" I asked in a mocking tone.

"Bitch, you act like a piece of fuckin' paper 'posed to mean some shit to me!"

I flinched at his unexpected tone. Without deliberation, I quickly reached into my purse for my cell phone to call 911—however, I quickly realized that Silk was still holding on to it. Instead I pulled out the next best thing: a four-inch automatic switchblade. I never left home without it.

"Silk, get the fuck away from me. I'm not playing," I warned him. I was trying to appear tough with the weapon in my hand, but my voice had betrayed me after cracking. Silk could see right through my façade. He knew I was scared as shit.

Holding his arms outstretched as if welcoming an attack, he asked, "Fuck you gon' do? Stab a nigga?" He suddenly tossed my phone to the ground and took a few steps away from me. "Don't worry, Cam. You gon' see me again. You gon' be seein' a lot of me since you all by yaself now," he laughed. Shaking his head at me, he walked towards his truck.

I instantly wondered what the hell he meant when he referred to me being all by myself. Suddenly, my wheels started turning. He couldn't have possibly known Jude would get arrested tonight. Could he?

As I watched Silk pull off in his white Denali, I suddenly came to the horrifying conclusion that he undeniably had something to do with Jude being arrested tonight.

***

Jude was being held down at the Cleveland County Jail in downtown Cleveland. Not even twenty-four hours since Jude's booking and prison intake process had elapsed before I was down there to bail him out. After paying ten percent of his bail, he was finally relinquished from the County's custody.

I had barely given him a chance to get a whiff of fresh air before I began barraging him with questions. "Are you gonna talk to me, Jude—"

"Cam, not right now. I got a lot of shit on my mind," he said in an irritated tone.

"Well, I feel like I at least deserve an explanation—"

"Cam, I said not right now," he repeated in a stern tone.

I hesitantly chalked up the fact that Jude wouldn't fill me in on what was happening with him. And instead of pressing on, I decided to simply drop it…for now.

"Did you ever get in touch with Jerrell?" Jude asked before climbing into the truck.

"He never answered his phone," I informed him. His older brother Jerrell lived in Columbus, Ohio which was two hours away from Cleveland. There was no other way for me to get in contact with him besides calling him. Hell, he didn't even have a Facebook that I could hit him up on.

Jude sighed dejectedly. "This shit crazy," he said to himself.

It was apparent that whatever trouble he was in was taking a toll on him. I just wished he'd talk to me about it. It was to my understanding that we had already established trust in our relationship, so I didn't see why Jude felt the need to keep things from me…However, I couldn't be too hypocritical. After all there was no way in hell I was going to tell Jude that Silk was most likely involved in him being arrested in the first place.

For the remainder of the ride home, we avoided small talk. Even after we stepped foot inside the house, there wasn't much Jude had to say. His distant behavior had definitely caused my suspicions to rise but as of now I would leave well enough alone.

Jude had just stepped into the master bathroom and closed the door behind him when suddenly my cell phone rang. I rolled my eyes once I recognized the familiar number displayed across the cracked touch screen.

"What do you want?" I asked through gritted teeth.

"I just wanna talk—"

Click!

I hung up the phone before Silk had a chance to finish his statement. As expected, he called me right back. This time I allowed the voicemail to pick up. Like the pest he was, he sent a text message seconds after. However, that I didn't ignore. After unlocking my phone, I read the incoming text message I had just received:

Meet me at PB tmrw nite.

I didn't bother responding to his text message. However, two minutes later he sent a second one that read: *It's important.* Before I could respond to that, he quickly replied with: *It's about ya dude. Trust me bay u gone wanna hear this shit.*

Suddenly, the shower water had begun running. Ultimately, I had two options: Either meet Silk down at Pandora's Box—the club he danced at— to see what exactly he was talking about or I could simply ignore and avoid him altogether. On the other hand, I didn't like being faced with the unknown. Nevertheless, I didn't give Silk the benefit of the doubt. If I showed up, I showed up. If I didn't, I didn't. It was as simple as that.

***

"Where're you going?" Jude asked the following night.

I had just slipped my feet into a pair of sequin floral flats when he had asked. It was going on seven o'clock p.m. and I had only one destination in mind. Nevertheless, I said, "I'm going to meet my girl, Tiffany up at Richmond Square. We might go to Southgate Lanes afterward. Is that cool?"

In all actuality, I hadn't seen or spoken to Tiffany in quite some time. We hit each other up on Facebook from time to time but that was about it. We were both too busy enjoying our own summer vacation to keep the promise of staying in touch with one another.

Jude sat up in our king size platform bed and rested his back against the button-tufted headboard. Patting the empty space beside him, he ushered for me to join him. "Come here real quick, bay," he said in a soothing tone.

I slowly made my way over towards him and plopped down on the edge of the bed beside him. He wrapped his strong arms around my tiny waist and pulled me close.

"You look nice," he complemented.

Keeping it pretty simple, I was dressed casually, wearing a pair of khaki cuffed pleated shorts and a white racerback tank top.

I laughed modestly. "Thanks, bay."

Jude sighed. "Look, I know I been acting funny lately, but I just been really stressed out about the court date and everything. I mean, they hit me with some shit." He paused and I patiently waited for him to continue and hopefully fill me in on what was going on with him. "You need a couple dollars or you good?" he simply asked.

Sighing inwardly, I quickly stood to my feet and grabbed my Matelassé clutch off the night stand. "I'm good," I answered in an irritated tone before walking out the bedroom. Initially, I felt bad for what I was about to do, but Jude was giving me no other choice.

Thirty minutes later, instead of pulling into the vast parking lot of Richmond Town Square Mall, I was instead pulling into Pandora Box's crowded parking lot. I knew Jude wouldn't be thrilled if he knew that I was here but I was all too curious to hear what Silk had to say.

After parking my car, I killed the engine and hopped out. I could hear the music inside of Pandora's Box bumping from outside. It seemed like only yesterday when Silk had been shot in the parking lot by Tank—an old fling from the past and former dancer at Pandora's Box.

At the doors, I was met by a hefty, ball-head bouncer. He wore a black shirt with the word security printed in white across his chest. Coincidentally, he was also a male dancer here at Pandora's Box but tonight he was playing the unexciting role of a security guard.

After checking my clutch for any dangerous items, I showed my identification card and paid the five dollar cover fee.

The moment I entered Pandora's Box, the lights were already dimmed and it was apparent that I had just walked in during a performance.

Suddenly, a shirtless male dancer walked into the center of the club. Dozens of horny—most likely married—women began clapping and cat calling upon his entrance. The tall, brown skinned dancer wore a pair of black cargo pants. His face was covered by a custom-made full head black and silver mask. In his right hand was a leather whip and from the way he was circling the stage in an enticing stride, I could tell he was scoping the crowd for his victim of choice.

There were a few other male dancers working the floor and mingling with women. I didn't see Silk among them. I figured he was still in the dressing room preparing for his upcoming performance.

The Weeknd's "What You Need" played through the speakers and the dancer effortlessly made his chest muscles bounce to the beat. For a minute, I forgot why I was even here. I was so engrossed in the show, that Silk had been momentarily pushed to the back of my mind.

Snapping myself back to reality, I headed towards the dressing room—as odd as it sounded women *were* actually allowed back there and some even offered "inspiration" for the male dancers. Just as I was making my way through the horny spectators, I suddenly felt someone grip my elbow. However, it wasn't a firm or forceful grip.

The moment I looked up, I stared into the masked face of the male dancer. He softly tugged on my elbow, signaling for me to join him on stage—which was basically the center area of the club.

Suddenly, everyone in the club's attention became fixated on me. Some women stared at me in envy, wishing they could be the chosen one. Others looked on with questioning glances, probably wondering if I would even allow whatever the dancer had in mind to happen.

I shook my head. "I can't—"

He softly placed a gloved finger against my lips and gently pulled my body into his. "Ssh. Just relax." His voice came out a little muffled behind the mask, nevertheless it sounded very familiar.

Before I was able to decline his offer, he swiftly lifted me off the ground and hoisted me in the air. He placed my legs over his shoulders and quick spun me around in circles. Scared for dear life, I clutched his head, fearful that he might just drop me.

As crazy as it sounded, even though I had dated Silk, he had never pulled me onto the stage to entertain with him. I was used to and comfortable with him choosing random women from the crowd. After all it was his job, and I would much rather prefer not to be put on the spot light anyway. I got enough of that at my old job. Understandably, I did not know what to expect from this mysterious dancer.

"Watch him ladies! Watch him!" The DJ yelled into the microphone.

With his face buried deep into my crotch, he spun me around several more times as women cheered on and threw bills onto the stage. After what seemed like the tenth spin, he finally lowered me down to waist level. Dizzy as hell, I had no choice but to wrap my legs around his waist to keep myself from falling.

"Just relax. I got you, baby," he whispered before lowering me onto the stage floor. Evidently, he noticed my uptightness.

After settling between my thighs in the "missionary" position, he began grinding and gyrating his erection against my crotch. The fabric of my khaki shorts was so thin that it felt like his actual dick was pressing against my clit. My cheeks flushed in embarrassment as I slowly found myself enjoying the tease.

"Get that shit! Get that shit!" the DJ was hyping up his performance and the women absolutely loved it.

The Weeknd crooned through the massive speakers as the male dancer continued to seduce me. "*He's what you want. I'm what you need.*"

What are you doing girl, I asked myself.

In a daring attempt to escape his seductive act, I tried to ease from underneath him, but the minute I tried, I realized what a big mistake I had made. He quickly intertwined his strong legs around mine and effortlessly flipped me onto my stomach. Before I was able to gather what the hell kind of move he had just executed, he grabbed my waist and began pumping vigorously against my ass.

"That's right! Show her ass who in charge! Don't run from the dick! Take it!" the DJ yelled into the microphone.

The women absolutely loved the act and quickly flocked the stage to make it rain on us.

Once the women exited the stage, the mysterious dancer finally helped me to my feet. "See that wasn't so bad, now was it?" he asked.

Suddenly, I thought back to the first night I had met Jude at The Playpen in Columbus, Ohio. He was so uptight and stuck up acting that night. He didn't even want a lap dance. A *paid* lap dance at that!

I sighed inwardly. *Jude*, I thought. He'd be pissed beyond a reasonable doubt if he knew I was even here. Gathering what little pride I had left, I headed towards the dressing room.

"Going to change them underwear, huh?" A random woman teased as I rushed past her.

Chapter 3

I pushed open the stiff wooden door that led to the men's dressing room—I was instantly met with the unexpected sight of Silk snorting a line of coke at the counter.

We were the only two in the dressing room and I quickly cleared my throat making my presence known. Silk, however, wasn't surprised when he looked up and noticed me standing there. He knew I'd show up.

I pointed to the residue left on the counter from the line he had just done. "When did you start doing that?" I asked in a non-confrontational tone.

"What it matter? You ain't my bitch," Silk noted.

I could not believe the same man who had choked me out, assaulted me and damn near planned out Pocahontas' execution was behaving in such a childlike manner. All because he was upset at the fact that I was now someone else's woman.

Usually he was such a hard ass but he had allowed his jealousy to degrade him to behaving like a mere child, upset that he couldn't get his way.

I propped my hands on my hips. "Look, Silk…what did you want to talk to me about?" I asked. I didn't have time for the games, I wanted to get straight down to the nitty gritty. I was disregarding my own restraining order by even being here. "What do you have to tell me that was so important, you couldn't just say it on the phone," I pressed on. "You talk on the phone any other time," I pointed out. Especially since I knew it was him who had been playing on my cellphone the past few days.

Silk snorted and wiped away any residue that was left around his nostrils. Pulling his seat out slightly, he turned around to face me. The only stitch of clothing he wore was a pair of black Hanes boxers, but even that sight alone wasn't enough to excite me like it used to. I used to melt at the very touch of Silk. Just the sight of him used to stimulate me. Now all it did was make me sick.

"I been fuckin' with this broad that comes up to the show every now and then," Silk said.

I made a face. "And? What that got to do with me?" I asked nastily.

"She works down at the police station on 93rd." Silk was slowly but surely filling in the pieces to the puzzle. "I had her look up some info on ya boy," he sneered. "You laid up with a nigga you know 24ancing' about."

"What do you mean?" I asked. I was asking it but in my heart I wasn't sure if I was ready to hear it and accept it.

"I bet you ain't know about ya boy's little car operation, huh?" Silk snickered. "Ya Mr. Mothafuckin Perfect ain't so perfect at all," he taunted.

"So you really did call the police, huh, Silk? Why would you do that?"

"'Cause I knew that nigga was gon' get knocked. I been told ya ass to end it but you ain't wanna listen. Bitch, if I can't have you, I'ma be damned if I let the next mothafucka have you."

Silk was talking crazy but suddenly, everything was beginning to make sense. Jude had no idea he was going to get arrested that night. If I had to guess, I'd bet money Silk had followed us from Shooters and waited for the perfect opportunity to call the police.

"I'll let ole' dude fill you in on the details and shit," Silk said. "I just wanted to give you a heads up on the nigga you *think* you in love with." He stood to his feet and pulled on a pair of black leather chaps.

I stood a few feet away from him in silence as I digested his words. After pulling on a black cowboy hat, Silk walked past me. "At least you knew about the dirt I was doin'," he said before exiting the dressing room.

For several seconds, I simply stood there in silence, marinating on his words. I was pissed that he would even take the initiative to find dirt on Jude, but I was mostly upset with Jude for not being real with me.

After collecting my thoughts, I quickly left the dressing room. Silk was dancing at a nearby table. Women were waving their bills around as they eagerly anticipated their turn to receive attention.

Chris Brown's "Sweet Love" was now bumping through the speakers as Silk took to dancing on a Caucasian heavy set female. I watched as he took her plump hand and guided her fingers down his oily chest. For a brief moment, I allowed myself to reminisce about the good memories Silk and I once shared. Like every other relationship, we went through our share of turmoil but we also had our good moments. Once upon a time, I couldn't even imagine myself being happy with anyone else but Silk. I was just that gone over him.

The chubby white woman continued to fan her bills in Silk's face as she enjoyed her free feel. She even went as far as to try and slip her hand inside his briefs. Apparently, she was feeling herself a little too much off the Moscato she was sipping on.

Suddenly and just as unexpectedly, Silk snatched the bills from the woman's hands. "Gimme this shit, bitch!" he yelled. "You sittin' up here flashin' the shit in my face! I ain't 25ancing' for my mothafuckin' health!"

The women at the table were instantly startled by Silk's sudden temperament. A couple even screamed and one even slid her chair away from the table as though she feared Silk might actually start swinging.

The record scratched and the music instantly subsided. The DJ quickly left the booth to see what the hell was going on.

Another male dancer—known as Foreplay—rushed over towards Silk to calm him down.

I had never seen Silk behave this way at work. But then again, he had seemingly turned into a whole new man since our breakup. Don't get me wrong he was never the perfect, sweet gentleman most of these women here believed him to be. He was possessive, controlling, and at times even abusive. Nowadays he was thrice as bad. Hence, the restraining order I had to file against him some months ago.

"Aye, man, what are you doing?! Chill!" Foreplay placed his hand on Silk's chest.

"Naw, man! Fuck this shit, man!" Silk pointed his finger in the frightened white woman's face. "This bitch tryin' to play me!"

"Dude, ain't nobody tryin' to play you." Foreplay pulled Silk away from the woman. "You trippin,' dog!"

The DJ quickly came over in order to deescalate the situation. "Look, Silk, why don't you just go home for the night. You obviously stressed out, bruh. I don't want you scarin' none of the women away."

The DJ's sister owned Pandora's Box and whenever she was not in attendance during the shows, he also served as an overseer.

Silk violently shook Foreplay off. "Nigga, this some bullshit!" He motioned towards his surroundings. "All this shit some bullshit!" Silk headed towards the dressing room furious at the fact that he was being asked to leave. "*Damn*!" Silk screamed before kicking an empty chair over.

I shook my head at the unbelievable scene that I had just witnessed. Silk was like a total stranger now…and I assumed his new drug of choice had a lot to do with his odd behavior.

Since there was nothing else left to see, I headed outside towards my truck. As soon as I pressed the door unlock button on the car remote, I heard the sudden sound of footsteps approach me from behind.

Turning on my heel, I watched as Silk jogged up to me. "Hold up real quick!" he said.

Damn, this nigga dressed fast as hell, I thought. Anyway, I ignored him as I opened the driver door.

"Hold on, Cam. Damn, I just wanna talk to you real quick." In a matter of seconds, Silk rounded the truck and climbed into the passenger side.

"What, Silk?! What do you want?" I lashed out.

"Cam, I just wanna talk to you…and it ain't even about that nigga. It's about us—"

"It ain't no fuckin' us!"

"You still gon' keep this charade up? Now look, I done put up with this bullshit long enough. I told you before to end that shit. You ain't listen—"

"Silk, when are you ever gonna accept that the fact that it ain't never gonna be an 'us' again?" I asked.

Silk's voice took on a softer tone as he spoke. "How you expect me to just get over you?" he asked. "You were the only female I ever cared about. Pure, Poca…all them hoes…they wasn't shit but some easy pussy. You meant everything to me. I ain't never felt the way I feel about you with no other bitches," Silk professed. "A nigga can't live without you, Cameron. I still love you. And you a fuckin' lie if you say you still don't love me too."

Silk reached over in attempt to caress my cheek but I quickly pulled away. I couldn't stand to even hear him utter Pocahontas' name after what he'd done. The night Pocahontas had been murdered was painted crystal clear in my mind. She had robbed Kevin—a guy whom she'd met at Smoove's and turned tricks with occasionally. Silk, being the coldhearted bastard that he was, pointed Kevin right in the direction to find Pocahontas.

It seemed like only yesterday, me and Pocahontas was chilling in her Challenger. It was then that'd I seen her vulnerable side for the first—and last—time. Just as Pocahontas and I were sharing our moment of truth, we were suddenly rammed from behind by a van. Kevin sent Poca's Challenger spiraling out of control and before I knew it, I had been knocked unconscious.

When I finally came to, I had witnessed the horrifying scene of Kevin letting loose two bullets into Pocahontas's body. Strangely, Kevin decided to spare me…

My tear ducts stung as I felt the oncoming tears approaching. Blinking them away, I looked over at Silk in resentment. The most fucked up thing out of the whole situation was that Pocahontas was Silk's baby mother.

"So you tellin' me you don't miss me at all?" Silk asked.

"No. I don't," I answered through gritted teeth.

Silk leaned over in the passenger seat towards me and I quickly jumped back afraid of what his next move might be. You never knew when it came to him. The back of my head collided with the window and I realized there was nowhere to go.

"So you don't miss the way I used to beat that shit up?" Silk whispered. "You don't miss the way I used to suck on that pussy?"

Playing the sex card was usually my weakness when it came to Silk but it damn sure wouldn't work now. "Silk, don't do that," I told him.

"That nigga hit it how I used to?" Silk licked his full lips for good measure.

"Silk—"

Tap! *Tap*! *Tap*!

Silk and I quickly turned our attention towards the figure standing at the driver door.

"Well, I'll be damned," Silk smiled.

Jude tugged on the door handle but it wouldn't budge since the doors were locked.

"Open the damn door, Cameron. Get out the car!" he yelled.

I had never seen Jude this upset before but then again who could blame him? He had just caught me in the parking lot of a male strip club, in the car with my ex, of all people.

Silk wasted no time as he hit the door unlock button from his side. He climbed out before me, obviously welcoming an altercation. I took my time climbing out because I wasn't sure I even had an excuse already thought out.

The minute my foot touched the gravel, Jude went ham on me. "You know what?! I knew it was gon' be some funny shit goin' on between you and this nigga. You up here in my shit—the shit that I brought you with this mothafucka?!" Jude yelled. "I can't believe you, Cam. I really thought you were different." Jude's tone was laced with pain.

"Believe it, my nigga," Silk arrogantly chimed in.

Jude took one look at Silk and immediately lost it! Without warning, Jude charged at Silk full speed and shoved the hell out of him. Silk instantly lost his footing, stumbled, but quickly regained his balance.

"*Jude, stop*!" I screamed.

But it was no use, they were already posted up. Silk threw the first punch but Jude quickly ducked the blow. They grabbed one another and began scuffling right there in the parking lot. After wrestling for several seconds, Silk managed to get in a quick jab that connected with Jude's jaw and sent him to the ground.

Silk charged at Jude while he was down, but Jude quickly jumped off the ground and scooped Silk up by his legs in an attempt to drop him. He effortlessly lifted Silk off the ground and slammed him into a nearby Hyundai Sonata.

Suddenly, the bouncer ran over towards the altercation, with a few male dancers in tow. Jude managed to get in a good few blows that caused Silk to stagger and fall to the ground. The bouncer grabbed Jude before he was able to get at Silk again.

"Aye! Aye! *Chill*!" the bouncer ordered.

Jude violently snatched away from the bouncer. "*Fuck off me*!" he yelled. He stormed over towards his black 2012 Fisker Karma.

I quickly walked over towards him. "Jude?" My voice cracked.

He held his hand up in a dismissive way. Obviously, he didn't want to be bothered but I couldn't be mad at him. I watched in silence as he climbed into his car and peeled off.

Silk's fellow male dancers helped him to his feet and made sure he was okay but his health was the last thing on his mind. His gaze connected with mine, but I quickly looked away and headed towards my truck.

"Cameron?!" Silk called out. "Cameron, don't fuckin' walk away from me!"

I ignored Silk as I hopped into my truck and pulled off.

***

I barely got a chance to stick my key into the keyhole before the front door swung open.

"Yo, I can't fuckin' believe you, dude!" Jude yelled.

"You didn't even give me a chance to explain." I walked around him into our condo.

"It ain't shit to explain! You went from supposed to be going to kick it with ya girl but instead I find you in the car with this nigga! You know what?! I don't understand ya'll fuckin' women." Jude shook his head. "You bitch and complain about how it ain't no good niggas, but when you finally get one, you fuck it up!"

I whirled around and faced Jude. "Hold up. Let's talk about you for a minute, Jude!" I countered.

"What about me?!"

"When were you ever gonna tell me the truth about your *business*?" I made air quotes using my fingers.

"What are you talking about?" Jude asked.

I walked up to him and looked him dead in the eye. "The little car scheme you got going on," I clarified. "When were you ever going to tell me the truth?"

Jude's cheeks turned beet red. His jaw muscles tensed. "I ain't think I owed you an explanation," he simply said. "Shit, whatever I'm doing is my damn business. I'm taking care of me and mine and that's all that matters. The details ain't important."

"What do you mean they're not important?" I argued.

"I'm sayin,' what I'm doin' shouldn't even matter to you. I take care of you. You ain't strippin' no more. Fuck it matter how I'm getting' money?!"

I almost didn't even recognize Jude from the way he was talking. Silk was absolutely right about one thing. I was laid up with a man I seemingly knew nothing about.

"And besides, how the hell you know all this?" Jude asked.

I folded my arms. "It doesn't matter," I mocked him.

"I mean shit, I ain't perfect if that's what you been thinking all this time," Jude said. "I'm sorry to fuckin' disappoint you, baby girl."

"You could've been upfront and honest with me from day one," I told him. "So what was it that you were doing? Scamming people? Selling busted up cars? Giving people phony titles?" I was just throwing accusations out there while hoping for the truth to eventually surface.

"Man, it ain't none of ya business." Jude walked around me and it was clear that I was obviously frustrating him. Suddenly, he stopped in his tracks and turned to face me. "And instead of askin' me all these damn questions why don't you just try supportin' me and holdin' me down for whatever might happen. That's what a real woman would do, Cam. Not runnin' to her ex whenever—"

"I didn't run to him!"

"Well why the hell did I catch ya ass in the car with him?!" he asked." I mean seriously, Cameron, do you understand the dynamics of what we have? Why would you wanna fuck that up?"

My tone instantly softened. "Jude—"

"Why the hell would you put us in this situation?"

"I didn't mean to, baby. I was just trying to—"

"You shouldn't be trying anything when it comes to that nigga! He doesn't mean you any good, Cameron. You saw what happened last time when he popped up and hear you go again! Do you even want something different from that no good ass nigga?" he asked. "Because right now you showin' me that you ain't ready," he said. "Do you wanna keep running back to that nigga? Is that what you want?"

I quickly opened my mouth to defend myself but Jude however cut me off. "Man, whatever. I don't even wanna know. I can't even talk to you right now. I'm finna go outside and smoke."

I watched as he walked out the condo and slammed the front door behind him. I was just about to follow him out the door when suddenly his cell phone rang on the end table. Disregarding my better judgment to not answer his phone, I picked it up.

The caller ID indicated that it was his cousin, Tez. "Hello," I answered on the second ring.

"Cameron? What's up, is Jude around? I gotta holla at him about some important shit."

"Is everything okay?" I asked concerned.

"Hell naw. I just found out that Jerrell got indicted. Nigga been locked up all week and his bond got denied," Tez explained. "I'm just now hearing about this shit. I think they might've put a warrant out for Jude's arrest too."

Wow, I thought. That explained why I couldn't get in touch with Jerrell the night Jude had been arrested.

"One second," I said. "Let me go get Jude."

I quickly headed outside, where I found Jude sitting on the bottom step freaking a Black and Mild.

"Baby—" My sentence was instantly cut short as I watched Silk's white Denali pull hastily into our parking lot.

"The fuck?" Jude quickly stood to his feet.

Jude's cell phone slipped from my fingers and crashed into the ground, breaking upon impact.

Silk instantly hopped out his truck, not bothering to put it in park. His truck continued to roll along, with no one behind the wheel, before it crashed into a neighbor's red Ford F-150.

Suddenly, everything happened all at once. Silk snatched the silver glock from his waistband and took aim at me!

It was right then and there that I saw my life flash before my very eyes…

Chapter 4

Pop! *Pop*! *Pop*!

The loud gunshots rang throughout the night air. One bullet shattered our living room window—Jude quickly turned around and grabbed me before taking two bullets to the back! Together we both fell to the pavement, with Jude's limp body landing on top of me.

The next thing that happened surprised the hell out of me. Silk brought the loaded Glock to his temple. His gaze never faltered…Suddenly, he pulled the trigger!

Pop!

I screamed at the exact same moment that Silk's body dropped to the pavement. His cold eyes were wide open as he stared at me from several feet away. A large pool of dark red blood slowly formed beneath his head.

Tears streamed from my eyes before I quickly turned away. I gently rolled Jude over onto his back. I checked his pulse and was relieved to see that he was still alive.

"*Somebody help me*!" I screamed. "*Somebody*?!"

***

Jude was unresponsive as he was rushed into the hospital on an EMT stretcher. I tried to follow him to wherever they were taking him but instead I was stopped by a nurse and informed to wait in the waiting room until further notice.

Not being able to be by his side was killing me. Suddenly, I felt bad that our last moments together had been filled with arguing and bickering. If Jude didn't make it out of this okay, I didn't know if or how I would ever be able to forgive myself.

After speaking with the police and providing a statement, I was finally greeted in the waiting room by Jude's doctor. He informed me that Jude's bullets were removed but that he was currently in critical condition and I would not be able to visit him as of now.

Choking back tears, I accepted what he had said and hesitantly made my way home. Alone.

Yellow caution tape outlined the perimeter of the Clifton Pointe Condos, and served as a painful reminder of what had just taken place. There were even a few officers still on the scene, gathering statements from the residents. As I headed to my loft, I made a mental note to have our window replaced first thing in the morning.

***

I didn't bother showering or even removing my bloodied clothes as I climbed into the queen size bed and pulled the sheets over me. After crying for what felt like hours, I finally managed to doze off for a brief period. However, I didn't get much sleep. After waking up in the middle of the night in a cold sweat after having a nightmare about Silk's suicide, I tossed and turned until the sun rose. When it finally did I took a quick shower and called the window repair service. After throwing on some comfortable clothes, I headed to the hospital to see if Jude's condition had finally stabilized.

It only took about ten minutes to get to the Cleveland Clinic in Lakewood. To my dismay, the entire parking lot was packed to capacity. Taking my chances, I decided to park on the street. There were a few other cars parked there also and I didn't see a ticket on any of them so I figured I was cool.

After speaking with the employee at the front desk, I headed upstairs to Jude's room which was located on the tenth floor. He was no longer in the Intensive Care Unit and had been moved into his own room. Fortunately, his condition was now stable and he was finally allowed visitors.

I said a silent prayer to myself as I waited for the elevator to come down. After all, I could only hope and pray for the best as far as his health and recovery.

None of this shit would have even happened if I didn't take my ass up there to see Silk, I cursed myself. I couldn't help but feel that everything that had happened was my fault.

The elevator chimed before the doors slowly opened. In less than six months, I had gone from visiting Silk in the hospital to visiting Jude in the hospital. Talk about an unfortunate turn of unexpected events.

When I finally made it to Jude's room, I noticed that I was not his only visitor. His mother—along with some young light skinned female—was situated on either side of Jude's hospital bed.

I had met Jude's mother only once during a family reunion a couple months ago. She was pretty sweet then but I doubted her take on me would ever be the same considering it was mostly my fault that her son was even in the hospital to begin with. If I hadn't taken my ass up to Silk's job in the first place, none of this crazy shit would have ever happened.

Besides the consistent beeps from the heart monitor, the room was completely silent as they sat beside a sleeping Jude.

I didn't know if it was my place to intrude or not but I was Jude's girlfriend after all and I felt I had every right to see him as well. Clearing my throat softly, I tapped on the door and politely made my presence known.

They both looked over in my direction. Jude didn't have any sisters so I couldn't help but wonder who this chick was. Her light skin tone hinted that she was obviously biracial. Black and

Caucasian if I had to guess. She had pouty pink lips, beautiful gray eyes, and her curly sandy brown hair was piled to the top of her head in a wild but cute bun.

Who is she, I thought.

"Hey, I—I'm Cameron," I stammered. "…Jude's girlfriend."

"I know who you are," Jude's mother's voice was cold and emotionless as she spoke. "But if you don't mind, we'd like to have some privacy. Why don't you come back later," she suggested in a nasty tone.

I was slightly taken back by her demeanor but I could not blame her nonetheless. I only wished she understood that I cared about Jude just as much as she did and I didn't mean for any of this to happen.

"I…um…okay," I stuttered before backing up out of the room. She wanted her privacy and I had no choice but to grant her request.

I was making my way back towards the elevators when suddenly I felt an arm gently grab my shoulder.

"Um, excuse me?"

I turned on my heel and was surprisingly met with the same pair of wide gray eyes from only moments ago. "Yes?" I asked as politely as I could even though I was irritated as hell.

"Hello, my name is Ericka. I'm a good friend of the family," she explained in a syrupy sweet voice that almost made me sick. "I'm also Jude's ex-girlfriend."

My heart instantly sank into the pit of my stomach. *Here we go*, I thought.

"See, I just came back home from the Air Force," she explained. "And um…well…I'll just get straight to the point," she said. "Um…about what Mrs. Patterson said about coming back later…" Her voice suddenly took on a threatening tone. "How about you just not come back at all?"

I propped a hand on my hip and looked this yellow bitch up and down. "Excuse me?"

Ericka took a few steps closer to me. She towered over me by at least five or six inches but I did not feel intimidated in the least. "You heard me," she said. "Stay. Away. From. Jude." She paused between each and every word she said to ensure that I heard her loud and clear. "He doesn't need a troubled bitch like you in his life. Hell, look where he's ended up." She gestured towards our surroundings.

She smirked a little and I really wanted to slap it off her face. I didn't know who the hell she thought she was.

"Hold up. Look—"

"No, you look and listen," she said nastily. "Keep your ass away from Jude. Or else I'd hate to see you end up in the room beside him," she threatened.

Oh hell no, I thought. No this bitch didn't just go there!

I quickly opened my mouth to say something. Suddenly Mrs. Patterson peered into the hallway and stopped me from saying a mouthful. "Hurry, Ericka! Jude's waking up!"

Ericka looked over her shoulder. "Coming, mama!" she said in that phony sweet voice of hers.

Mama?

She turned back to face me, gave me one last threatening glance and headed back towards Jude's room.

I had a feeling I would run into her ignorant ass on more than one occasion. She had another thing coming if she thought I was going to stay away from my man.

***

My day only went downhill after my brief but tense encounter with Ericka. The moment I reached my car, I noticed a bright yellow ticket shoved underneath my windshield wiper. Me and every other person parked on the street had just received a parking ticket.

After snatching the ticket from underneath the windshield wipers, I climbed into the truck and left. Ericka had a lot of damn nerve, and I couldn't help but to harp on her threatening words. She seriously had no damn right telling me to stay away from Jude. I couldn't wait to get some alone time with him so I could ask him about him and Ericka's past.

Chapter 5

Two days later.

The sounds of soft cries and whimpers sent an unsettling chill up my spine as I made my way down the narrow church aisle that led to Silk's black steel casket. Two funerals in less than six months—the first being my girl X-Rated's. She was an innocent bystander who was killed during a fatal shooting at the after hour spot known as Smoove's. Pocahontas would've been the third but her mother simply had her cremated. There wasn't even a memorial service held for her. Truthfully, I couldn't blame her mother. I honestly didn't think too many people—if anyone at all—would have shown up to Pocahontas' funeral. She had done so many people grimy.

When I reached Silk's casket, I almost didn't recognize the swollen figure lying in the open casket. He had entirely too much makeup caked on his face and overall, he did not look like the same man I had once been deeply in love with.

Never, in a million years, would I have expected to be attending his funeral. Silk never took me as the suicidal type. I still didn't even understand what his motive was for pulling the trigger on himself. Of course I knew the drugs had taken over and his frame of mind was shaky but I would've never guessed he would've taken his own life. Silk was looking for the ultimate vengeance and sure enough, he got it.

I opened my mouth to bid my last farewell but instead became choked up on my own tears of sorrow. I did not expect for this to be as hard as it was. Silk may have cheated on me, beat me, and hurt me in general but at the end of the day I had a lot of love for the man lying in this casket.

My vision quickly blurred from the oncoming tears. *I can't do this*, I thought as I quickly turned around—

Whap!

It felt like the wind had been knocked out of me as I fell to the floor! Silk casket rocked a little after I bumped into it on the way down. People immediately screamed and gasped at the unexpected blow. Blood leaked profusely from my nose and it took me several seconds to realize I had just been punched in the face.

Silk's sister, Tamika stood over me with pure hatred in her tear-filled eyes. "Bitch, you got a lot of nerve bringin' your ass here!" she screamed.

A few of her family members rushed over and intervened.

"Tamika, relax," her mother said in a soothing tone. "I invited her."

Silk's uncle, Benny helped me off the floor. I cradled my bloody nose, fearing that it might actually be broken.

"Why would you invite her, ma?!" Tamika screamed. "It's her fault Terrence is even laying in that fuckin' casket!"

Her words stung like fire searing my skin, but I knew deep down inside that her accusation was partly true.

"Shit," I muttered, wiping away the thick blood trickling down my chin.

"Yeah, bitch. Hurts don't it?!" she yelled. "Now you fuckin' see how I feel!"

"Come on, let's get you out of here," Benny said as he led me away.

Suddenly, Tamika snatched me up by a fistful of my hair! Women screamed and more family members rushed over to break the fight up.

My eyes burned with tears at the pain of my hair strands being torn from my scalp. "Tamika, stop!" I pleaded, clawing at her hands.

"*Tamika, let her go*!" her mother screamed.

"I'm gonna kill this bitch!" Tamika cried. "*She took my fuckin' brother from me*!"

"Tamika, let her go!" Benny yelled.

Tamika held a vice grip on my hair and it was apparent that she was not letting go without a fight. With her free hand, she pummeled my skull repeatedly, until my knees suddenly gave out beneath me.

Uncle Benny tried his hardest to pull me away. When the family members finally pried Tamika's fingers from my hair, she sent a devastating kick to my jaw with her four inch black heel!

My head instantly whipped back from the impact causing me to fall backwards. People were crying hysterically from the church gallery, while other family members were desperately trying their hardest to calm a kicking and screaming Tamika down.

Benny helped me to my feet and assisted me out of the funeral home. When we finally made it to the doors, he gently shoved me outside and closed the doors behind himself.

I had never felt so embarrassed in my life! My face was sore as hell and I could feel it swelling from the vicious assault Tamika had inflicted. Something told me not to come in the first place, but just like Silk's friends and family members, I wanted to pay my respects and bid him my last farewell. If I would've known that I would get pounced on in the process, I would have never showed up to begin with. The last thing I wanted to do was disrespect anyone.

Little did Tamika know, I was hurting just as much as she was. I loved Silk too.

With what little dignity and pride I had left, I dragged myself to my truck and prepared to return to an empty home.

I had a splitting headache by the time I made it home. What was supposed to have been a peaceful home going service had quickly turned into utter chaos. I had just had my ass handed to me by Silk's older sister, who understandably felt resentment towards me for her only brother's death.

Two days had elapsed since my run in with Ericka and my week was only getting worse. And if things couldn't get any more uncomfortable they surely did when I found Tiffany standing on my front steps. It wasn't so much as her being there, but it was the fact that I was still cradling my bloody nose. Obviously, I was embarrassed. I didn't want her seeing me like this.

Tiffany and I had both attended Cleveland State University. I would be returning for my junior year in the fall while she had finally obtained her two year degree in Accounting this year. To most she would probably be considered as a "goody goody" but she was pretty laid back for the most part. Before I met Pocahontas, we were once the best of friends. And she damn sure came through for me a lot in school. If it wasn't for Tiff, I don't think my ass would have ever made it off Academic Probation.

Tiffany took one look at my battered and bruised face and her mouth immediately fell open. "Oh my God, Cameron!" She skipped down the stone steps and ran towards me. "What the hell happened? Who did this to you? Did Silk do this to you?"

Tiffany was bombarding me with questions and I really did not feel like recounting the events that led up to the merciless ass kicking I had just suffered.

"What are you doing here, Tiff?" I asked instead. "You couldn't have called me before you stopped over?" Usually, I was never this brash but I really was not happy about her being here and seeing me like this. I felt totally caught off guard.

"Well…," she twiddled her thumbs. "Is it cool if we go inside so we can talk?"

I hesitated. "I guess," I finally agreed.

Tiffany followed me inside the condo and into the bathroom where I proceeded to nurse my bloodied nose. My blouse was covered in blood stains, my hair was in disarray and both of my eyes were blackened. I couldn't even look at myself in the bathroom mirror without cringing at my own reflection.

I turned the faucet on and ran a washcloth underneath the warm water. "What's up, Tiff?" I asked before wiping away the dried blood on my face.

"Well, you know I graduated and everything. I…um…," Tiff hesitated. "I thought it would be easier to get a job the minute I graduated but I haven't had much success," she explained. "My mom and I have been falling out nonstop. I've just been going through a lot lately…a whole bunch of stress." She sighed before pushing her glasses up on the bridge of her narrow nose. "I was…uh…wondering if I could stay here with you a while—just 'til I get on my feet," she quickly added.

I pinched my nostrils together and tilted my head back to stop the blood flow. "Tiff—"

"I mean I know I'm not working now but I am looking and the minute I find something, I swear—"

"Tiffany, it's cool," I waved her off. I had a splitting headache and I didn't even feel like talking or listening to her babble. "You can stay here," I told her. There was a guest bedroom and I didn't really want to be here alone with Jude in the hospital. It was super quiet, boring, and depressing in his absence. So although I wasn't crazy about Tiff being here it was better than being alone. Besides that, Tiffany had come through for me on countless occasions, letting me borrow her notes when I was too busy sleeping in class. I couldn't leave my girl hanging.

"So it's cool if I stay here?" Tiffany asked again as if she couldn't believe I was agreeing.

"Yeah, of course."

Tiffany shrieked, jumped up and down as if she had just hit the lottery and ran over towards me, pulling me into an embrace.

"*Ugghhh,*" I moaned in pain.

Tiffany quickly backed off. "Oh, I'm sorry, girl. I forgot."

Chapter 6

The following morning, while checking the mail, I noticed that Jude had received a letter from the IRS. Usually, I never went through his personal belongings, but he wasn't here and my nosiness was obviously getting the best of me.

After tearing the envelope open, my eyes quickly scanned the letter. "What the hell?" I muttered. "They're freezing his accounts?"

Jude was going to be pissed when he found out about this. And to top it off, the mortgage was due in two weeks. With his bank account frozen and me not working, I didn't know how the hell it was going to get paid. Tiffany couldn't contribute in the least and I didn't know what the hell to do.

Jerrell was locked up and I wouldn't dare ask Mrs. Patterson for a thing, especially considering that she now hated my guts.

I found Tiffany in the guest bedroom flipping through an old issue of *Seventeen*. I instantly doubted she was ever looking for a job as much as she said she was.

"Tiff, I'll be back," I told her.

She didn't even look up. "Okay," she answered absentmindedly.

After closing the door behind her, I headed outside. It wasn't until I started the truck up, that I noticed the gas needle was one notch from being on E. So much shit had been going on lately that it had completely slipped my mind to fill the tank up.

Five minutes later, I pulled into the Marathon gas station on Madison Avenue. After parking at pump two, I killed the engine and hopped out. Rummaging through my purse, as I made my way inside the gas station, I located two twenty dollar bills inside my wallet. Unfortunately this was all that was left of my spending money.

"You gotta be fuckin' kidding me," I mumbled.

Me and Jude's finances were all fucked up. The mortgage needed to be paid. Bills needed to be paid. There was no telling how much Jude's hospital bill would come up to. After all, medical insurance only covered so much of one's bill. Not to mention, the other living expenses…*What the hell am I going to do*, I thought.

Standing in line behind a heavy set older woman dressed in scrubs, I suddenly thought about Jude. Apart of me wanted to tell him about the letter from the IRS but I didn't want to upset him or add any stress especially during his recovery process.

"Can I help you?" the cashier asked, snapping me from my profound thoughts.

I handed her a twenty dollar bill. "Can I have ten on pump two?" I asked. *So much for filling the tank up*, I thought.

After being rang up, I headed outside to pump my gas.

The older heavy set woman in the scrubs was parked at pump three. The only reason I noticed her was because she kept staring at me every few seconds.

"Barbara," she suddenly said.

I turned and looked behind me to see if she was addressing someone else.

She pointed towards me. "You're Barbara's daughter. Kenny's kid, right?"

How the hell did this lady know who my parents were, I wondered.

She hung the nozzle up and began snapping her fingers as if she were trying desperately to recall something. "Camille…Chloe…"

"Cameron," I finally spoke up.

She snapped her finger a final time before making her way over towards me. "Cameron. That's right. I'm your father Kenny's sister, Linda," she explained. "I know you probably don't remember me. You're a little bitty girl the last time I saw you." She placed her hand at waist level to indicate how tall I was when she last saw me.

Linda looked like a darker version of my dad…or at least what I could remember of how he looked. I didn't have one picture of either of my parents.

"Oh, okay," I said nonchalantly. Where the hell was Aunt Linda when I was being bounced around from one orphanage to the next? I wasn't bitter. I was just saying.

"Well, I know you're in a rush to get where ever you gotta go and I'm on my way to the nursing home, so is it okay if I give you my number? I would love for us to rekindle. I really would like to get to know my niece if that's okay with you."

I rather wouldn't, I thought. But instead of telling her that, I plugged her number into my cell phone.

She stared at me with a dreamy look in her eyes for a few seconds before she spoke again, "Goodness," she sighed. "You look just like him," she said in regards to my father. She snapped herself from her thoughts. "Make sure you call me now," she told me before walking back towards her car.

"I will," I lied.

After hanging up the nozzle and screwing on the gas cap, I headed to the Cleveland Clinic.

Fortunately, Jude was all alone in his room. No Mrs. Patterson and thank God, no Ericka. Jude was asleep when I stepped inside. It was obvious they had him heavily medicated for the surgical pain.

Taking a seat in the hospital room chair beside Jude's bed, I gently reached for his hand and brushed my fingers over his knuckles. Had it not been for him shielding my body with his own, I probably wouldn't even be here.

Jude stirred softly before his eyes opened. "Hey, baby," he greeted in a muffled tone.

I brought his left hand to my lips and kissed his bruised knuckles. "How you feelin'," I asked?"

Jude groaned. "Shit, sore as hell." He tried to sit up but wasn't successful at it. "They talkin' bout keepin' me for a couple months."

"A couple months?!" I repeated in disbelief. I couldn't imagine us being apart for so long. Even though I could visit as much as I wanted, I missed his presence at home. I missed sleeping in the bed beside him every night.

"Yeah, observation and shit. Apparently, one of the bullets broke a bone in my rib cage. Not to mention, I got a damaged liver and—Cam, what's wrong?"

I couldn't help myself from bursting into hysterical cries. Tamika was right. All of this shit was my fault. "If I would've never went down there, none of this mess would've ever happened—"

"Sshh. Sshh," Jude said in a soothing tone. He gently caressed my cheek. "Hell, I'm alive ain't I?" He gave a weak smile. "Shit, could've easily been *two* homicides that night. But I'm here and you're here, baby," he said. "That's all I'm thankful for. It could've been worse."

"Yeah but—"

"Baby, I don't want you feelin' regretful," he said. "We ain't even gon' talk or think about that night. We just gon' move forward. You feel me?" he asked.

"Yes," I answered halfheartedly.

"What happened to your chin?" he asked, noticing the dark red bruise.

"I…uh…I burnt myself flat ironing my hair yesterday."

My hair looked an absolute mess. I had been too stressed lately to care the slightest bit about my appearance. Nevertheless, Jude brought my weak excuse.

"My mother notified the court and they pushed the court date back," he told me. "You gotta be strong for me, babe. I need you now more than ever," he said.

I met Jude's gaze.

"I'm sorry for not tellin' you the truth about me," he suddenly said.

I waved him off. "It's not important—"

"No, it is. It really is. Seriously, Cameron. You been real with me since day one and I owe you the same," he said.

"Bay, you really don't—"

"No, I wanna tell you," he said. "I *have* to tell you," he stressed. "That way when I do my time—which I know I'ma end up doin', I won't be sittin' back regrettin' that I ain't keep it real with you, you know?"

I didn't like the fact that he believed he would go to jail. I wanted him to have a little shred of hope like I did, but I assumed he was thinking realistically. After all, Jude was the "black and white" kind of person. He never saw a shade of gray.

" Me and Jerrell…," he hesitated. "We been…uh…doing this tax refund fraud shit for a couple years now. We were getting that paper too. I'm talkin' millions," he said. "We were using the refund money to buy cars for the lot," he admitted. "It wasn't never any car scheme shit we were running. Just thought we could outsmart the government. I mean, I knew the shit would catch up with us eventually…I just never thought it would so soon, you know?"

I thought about Pocahontas. "Well…everyone has to pay for their consequences someday" I said.

Jude sighed. "Shit…tell me about it."

"I do appreciate your honesty, babe…" My voice trailed off. I desperately wanted to tell him about his bank account being frozen. However, I thought better. Instead I decided to bring up Ericka. "Yeah, so…um…I met your lil' ex-girlfriend." I said sarcastically.

Jude looked out the hospital room's window. "Oh, yeah…Ericka?" he asked. "Yeah she told me she met you the other day." He looked back at me and smiled. "She said you were really sweet."

Sweet, I thought. This bitch had damn near threatened my life but she had the nerve to go back and tell Jude that I was *sweet*. I guessed that just showed how sheisty the bitch truly was. Either that or she was just flat out crazy. If I had to guess, I'd say the latter.

"So…um…I guess I'ma be seeing a lot of her, huh?" I asked.

Jude didn't miss the hint of sarcasm in my tone. "Baby, my mama invited her up here. She's only tryin' to be supportive."

"And is that it?" I asked in a serious tone.

"Yeah, babe. What you want me to say? You want me to tell her not to come up here?" he asked.

Yes.

Jude and I stared into each other's eyes for several seconds before I finally spoke. "Is there still something going on between you two?" I asked. I wanted to know the truth but at the same time I wasn't sure if I was exactly ready to hear the answer.

"What do you mean?" Jude asked dumbfounded.

Why do men have to play these damn games, I asked myself.

"You and Ericka," I said. "Is there something goin' on between ya'll two?" I repeated.

"Man, Cam, no!" Jude was obviously growing frustrated. "Where are all these questions comin' from? 'Cause she showed up here that means we gotta be fuckin' with each other?"

"I was just asking," I said. "I can ask, right?"

"Man, I guess." His response was nonchalant.

Jude's mood has obviously gone downhill at the mention of something going on between him and Ericka. I decided to shift the conversation to a less touchy subject. "I told my girl, Tiffany that she could stay at the condo with me until she got on her feet. I hope that's cool with you."

"Yeah, it's all good." Jude didn't sound like he cared one way or the other.

"I miss you," I admitted.

He finally cracked a smirk. "You don't miss me for real."

"Yeah, I do." I stood up over him and kissed him on the forehead." I miss you a whole lot."

Our lips met for a passionate kiss.

"You know when I get out, I ain't gon' be able to put in work like I usually do," he laughed.

"Boy, you thinkin' bout some damn sex," I laughed. "You need to be thinking about getting better so you can come home."

We gave each other one last kiss and I promised I would return tomorrow.

After leaving the premises, I made my way towards the truck in the hospital parking lot—

"*What the fuck*?!" I screamed. Examining the four slashed tires, I couldn't believe somebody had actually done this to my shit.

"Bitch, I told your ass to stay away from Jude!" I heard a familiar voice yell from behind me.

I quickly turned around and watched Ericka skirt off while bumping Rihanna's "Where Have You Been".

I took off running after her silver Toyota Camry. "*You fuckin' bitch*!" I screamed. "Don't let me catch your ass! I'ma fuck you up!"

Tears streamed from my eyes as I shouted out useless threats. It seemed like I couldn't get a break lately.

Catching my breath, I rummaged through my purse and pulled out my cell phone.

Tiffany answered on the third ring, "What's up, girl?" she greeted cheerfully.

"Girl, I need you to come and get me from up here at the Cleveland Clinic in Lakewood." I placed my free hand on my forehead and turned around to survey the damage. I couldn't believe that crazy bitch Ericka would violate me like this.

"Is everything okay, Cameron?" Tiffany asked in a concerned tone.

"Girl," I sighed. "I'll just tell you when you get here."

"Alright, I'm on my way now."

I quickly disconnected the call. “This be that bullshit,” I swore to myself. Ericka was behaving irrationally for someone who wasn’t dating Jude. He could say whatever he wanted, but I knew there was something going on between the two of them.

Chapter 7

On the way home, I quickly filled Tiffany in on everything that had taken place over a mere week. From Jude being arrested to Silk's suicide and eventually leading up to Ericka's crazy antics.

Tiffany pulled her car into my garage and killed the engine. "If it wasn't for bad luck, you wouldn't have any at all, Cameron."

I sighed before hopping out. "Tell me about it."

The minute I stepped into the condo, I noticed Jude's IRS letter was re-opened and lying on top of the kitchen counter. I clearly recalled placing the letter back into the envelope.

Tiffany walked past me and headed to the refrigerator where she retrieved a bottled water.

I know this bitch was not snooping through my shit, I thought. I picked the piece of paper up and held it up for her to see. "Damn, Tiffany. Nosey much?" I asked sarcastically. I had every right to curse her ass out about invading my privacy but I had bigger problems to worry about.

She nearly choked on the water. "Oh…I was…uh…"

"Snooping," I finished the sentence for her.

She took a seat at the breakfast bar. "So what are you gonna do as far as rent and bills and stuff?" she asked.

I sighed and ran my fingers through my unkempt hair. "Girl, I don't know."

"Hmm…" Tiffany placed a finger on her chin and pretended to be deep in thought. "Well…you could always go back to stripping," she suggested. "I got it!" she suddenly said. "Why don't we both start dancing?"

I had to do a double take to be sure that I was hearing my girl correctly. "You?" I asked. "Stripping?!" I had to control myself from laughing in my homegirl's face. Tiffany couldn't have weighed more than one hundred and twenty-five pounds with clothes on. She had no ass whatsoever and if I had to guess I'd say she was a B-cup at the most. She also wore a pair of thick framed glasses. To put it short, she definitely wasn't exotic dancing material.

"Yeah," Tiffany said. "We both obviously need money. What money is more convenient and easier to get than stripping money?" she asked.

I made a face and shook my head. I had promised Jude that I would never step foot inside of a strip club again, and I had been good on my word for the past several months. "I don't know, Tiff. You ain't never ever stripped before. How do you even know you ready for that life?"

Tiffany sucked her teeth and waved me off. "Come on now, Cameron. It's just dancing. How hard can it be?"

***

Vixen was facing horizontally as she held onto the bronze pole. Her sister, Chyna stood vertically on top of Vixen's body while pretending she was surfing the endless waves. The fellas absolutely loved the performance; bills flew from every which direction, raining down on the two beautiful women on stage.

"Damn," Tiffany said in awe. Her eyes widened in disbelief as she watched the acrobatic act.

"Just dancing, huh?" I teased.

Ray Jr's "I'm Looking" blared loudly through the massive speakers as Tiffany followed me into the dressing room.

"*Hypnotic*?!" Juicy yelled excitedly the minute I entered the dressing room. "I see somebody done came out of retirement! Yeah, girl, I knew ya ass couldn't stay away from this money for too long!"

"What's up, girl. What's up everybody?"

After all the females greeted me, I took the initiative to introduce Tiffany—who was standing by my side quiet as a mouse. "Hey ya'll, this my homegirl, Tif—Temptation," I quickly said.

"What's up, Temptation," everyone greeted in unison.

The females were extra friendly to Tiffany probably because they didn't see her as much of a threat with her petite frame and thick glasses. Don't get me wrong, Tiffany was a cute girl. With flawless mocha brown skin, full lips and a gorgeous smile, she was definitely capable of making a few heads turn. If I had to compare her to a celebrity, I'd say she resembled a more grown-up KeKe Palmer. Tiffany definitely had the whole good girl look going on.

"Tiff, lose the glasses after you get dressed," I advised her.
"Well, how am I gonna see?" she asked redundantly.

I shook my head. "Fine, Tiff. Whatever."

I was more concerned with my own fruitful endeavors for this evening to care about Tiffany's appearance. The mortgage would be due soon. There were still bills that needed to be paid. I had to shake my ass twice as hard if I planned on leaving with a reasonable amount of money.

I quickly changed into a hot pink one piece with rhinestones embedded along the hem. Tiffany moved at the pace of a snail as she changed into the black foil mini dress I had let her have. It was brand new and since I had never worn it, I figured she could have it. However, the dancing heels I had given her were far from new. They were the first pair of stripper heels I had ever owned. Although my foot prints were ingrained in the soles, they were still pretty sturdy and beggars couldn't be choosers in

Tiffany's case. Besides, there was no way in hell I was going to let her wear my pink platform light up shoes.

From time to time I would entertain Jude in the comforts of our bedroom.

Juicy walked up to me at the vanity and placed her hand on the small of my back. "By the way, girl," she whispered. "I heard about what happened to Silk. I'm really sorry—"

"I appreciate it, girl. But I'm just trying to move forward," I repeated Jude's comforting words. However, I knew it was easier said than done.

"I feel you, girl. Stay up," she said before exiting the dressing room.

"How do I look?" Tiffany eagerly asked once she was fully dressed.

Like a parent fixing their child's clothing, I adjusted the dress so that it fit perfectly on her petite frame. "Better. You look hot," I told her.

"Hypnotic? New girl? Ya'll want some of this?"

Champagne was doing a line of cocaine a few seats away from us at the vanity. She had offered us to do a line much like someone would offer a guest coffee or tea. Champagne was a decent-looking chick. She reminded me of Kaleena from Diddy-Dirty Money and even had her head shaved just like the singer.

"Nah, I'm good," I declined. I thought about the night I had witnessed Silk snorting cocaine and how it had drastically changed him. I wanted no part of it. "Alright, Tiffany you ready?" I asked.

Tiffany hesitated. "No, I'm gonna um…I'm still getting ready," she said. "I'm gonna…uh…do my makeup," she told me.

I gave her a suspicious look but figured she was just nervous since this was her first night. "Alright. I'll catch you outside."

"Alright, then."

Ahmad, the club owner, practically ran into me as I stepped out the dressing room. "Hypnotic, you're up next." He gave my ass a firm slap. "I missed you, girl. Please don't leave us again."

I couldn't make any promises. Besides Jude would flip if he knew my ass was even in here, but I had to do what I had to do. He wanted me to hold him down and that's what I was doing. Well…at least that's what I wanted to believe I was doing.

DJ Khaled's "Take It to the Head" bumped throughout the club as I made my way towards the stage.

Chyna held her hand out for me, as I made my way up the stairs. "Get it, bitch!" she playfully slapped my ass.

Bills were already raining down on me before I even gripped the bronze pole. I felt like an ex drug addict about to get high again after being clean for a brief period. I was scared, nervous and excited. I knew I shouldn't have even have been doing this shit but I was already here so what the hell? Shaking off my anxiety, I gripped the pole.

Damn, I miss Poca, I thought. Where was she at when I needed her to sneak me a much needed drink? A slight smirk tugged at my lips as I thought about the night she had spiked my drink. I could've killed her. And then she had the nerve to play innocent as if she had done nothing wrong. That was Poca for you.

Take it to the head...Don't think about it, be about it. Don't be scared…

Chris Brown's soulful voice sang the chorus; I slowly but surely fell into beat. As I was doing my thing on stage, I suddenly noticed a familiar face standing at the bar…I instantly stopped what I was doing once I recognized who I was staring at…

He stood about six feet two inches tall. Judging from his cocky physique it was obvious that he hit the gym up on the regular. His skin was the color of cinnamon and his wide chestnut eyes were accentuated underneath dark, thick eyelashes. His full beard was tapered and a pair of diamond earrings glistened in both his ears in the dimly lit club. Although he was a handsome guy, he always seemed to sport the same mean mug whenever I saw him.

How could I forget him? And why the hell would he even show his face here after what he had done? It felt like only yesterday when I had been staring into the very face of death, looking up into the dark barrel of a loaded Glock.

I knew him simply as Kevin. He hung out at the afterhour spot, Smoove's. I didn't know him personally but I knew that he and Pocahontas had kicked it from time to time, and that he often paid for the kitty cat. I had never socialized with him myself but I knew he was some big name hustler that had connects from Broadway to Lorraine Avenue.

I assumed since Kevin was a well-known dope boy that was what initially drew Pocahontas to him in the first place. As usual, her greed clouded her judgment and she ended up robbing him for twenty stacks. But indeed karma was a bitch, and Kevin came back for Poca's ass in the most vengeful way imaginable. One bullet to the chest and one to the dome. Sadly, her greed ultimately led to her demise.

Kevin was fraternizing with his homie at the bar. Obviously, he felt my intense gaze because he suddenly looked up at me on stage. The smile that was just pasted to his light brown face only moments ago quickly disappeared.

My heart rate instantly sped up with images of Poca's lifeless body flashing into my mind. I nearly vomited on stage as I recalled how her wig had been gruesomely pushed back from the impact of the second bullet.

The look in his eyes silently threatened me but for some reason I couldn't break away from the intense stare.

Suddenly, he turned away and gave his homie dap before leaving the club. I finally released the breath I'd seemingly been holding once he left.

Chapter 8

"Tiffany?! Tiffany?! Chill!" I demanded. "*Relax*!"

The night had finally ended and I was forced with the impossible task of trying to dress my inebriated friend.

I didn't know how or when Tiffany had managed to get herself pissy drunk. One minute she was cool; mingling with the fellas and I had even noticed her giving a few lap dances—she obviously had the hustle in her after all—but the next thing I knew she was stumbling and falling all over the place.

Luckily for her, I made her keep her money bag in her locker in the dressing room. Some of the dancers were so damn cutthroat that they'd wait for a fellow dancer to get sloppy drunk so that they could easily steal their money. I didn't want Tiffany to fall prey.

As I tried my best to dress my drunken friend, I came to the sudden conclusion that she was definitely not fit for this lifestyle. I could see that now. Once she finally sobered up, I planned on having a nice, little talk with her about finding a different means to get money. For example, a normal nine to five.

"*I am so fucked up, Cameron*!" Tiffany laughed. She was slumped over in a chair at the vanity as I attempted to unfasten her dancing heels.

"I can see that," I told her. "But can you please stay still? You nearly poked me in the damn eye with that heel."

"*Oh, you are ca-razay*!" Tiffany laughed.

"No, more drinking for you, Tiff," I told her.

"You good, Temptation?" Juicy asked as she pulled on her pair of retro Jordans.

"She's good," I told Juicy. "Just had one too many drinks."

Tiffany giggled. "That's not all I had."

I didn't know what the hell that meant, but I figured the liquor had her talking recklessly. Tiffany was so hammered that I didn't even bother trying to change her back into her normal clothes. I simply slipped her bare feet into her pair of all white Adidas and helped her stand up.

She instantly began staggering and I quickly placed her arm around my shoulder to help her with her balance. Grabbing my rolling suitcase, we headed to Tiffany's 2012 Nissan Altima which was parked across the street from The Shakedown.

"Where the hell are we?" Tiffany giggled as she wobbled alongside me.

"Yo, is she cool?" the bouncer asked as we walked past him.

I shook my head. "She's fucked up," I answered.

The bouncer quickly grabbed Tiffany just before she fell to the ground, practically taking me with her.

"I got her," he said before lifting her into his arms.

"Oh, wow. You're my knight in shining armor," Tiffany slurred.

The bouncer carried Tiffany to the car and placed her in the backseat. After tipping him twenty dollars, I decided to count my tips for the night right there in the car. Aside from the mortgage needing to be paid, I now had to worry about getting my truck towed from the hospital's parking lot and getting brand new tires.

I swear when I see Ericka again, I'm going to whup her ass, I promised myself. And speaking of Ericka, I had a bone to pick with Jude tomorrow. There was no way in hell that I was not going to tell him about the crazy tire slashing shit she had pulled earlier.

"Six hundred and ten…six hundred and eleven…six hundred and twelve?!" I asked in astonishment. "That's it?!" The mortgage was four times what I had made tonight. "It's cool," I told myself. The mortgage wasn't due for another two weeks and I knew I'd easily scrape up that money from dancing.

"Where are we going, Cameron?" Tiffany slurred from the backseat.

Beep! *Beep*!

I quickly turned my head in the direction of the vehicle that had just pulled alongside me. Four black silhouettes stared at me through the tinted windows of a black Ford Excursion. They were bumping Dom Kennedy's "My Type of Party".

The man on the passenger side rolled his window down. "What's up, ma? Me and my niggas tryin' to run that! You with it? We got bread!" he shouted.

I sucked my teeth and quickly started Tiff's car up. These niggas had another thing coming if they thought I was about to let them run a train on me and my homegirl. They had life all the way fucked up.

The minute I pulled off, they did also making sure to keep their truck at the exact same speed as my car.

The guy on the passenger side was hanging out the window like Tupac, with his arms outstretched and everything. "Aye! Why you actin' like that?!" he yelled.

My heart rate sped up once the driver of the truck inched his vehicle closer to mine as though he were planning on side swiping it.

"Chill the fuck out!" I screamed before veering to the right to avoid a collision.

"Woo! Woo!" Tiffany cheered in the backseat, completely oblivious to what was happening.

Suddenly, the truck swerved into my lane practically running me off the road!

"*Fuckin' stop*!" I screamed. Flashbacks instantly came to mind from when Kevin had rear-ended me and Pocahontas the night she had been killed.

The guy on the passenger side found the entire situation comical but I was scared for my damn life! It was obvious that I was dealing with a bunch of drunken idiots.

"Whew! Cameron, do it again!" Tiffany sang from the backseat.

"Tiff, shut the hell—*Ahh*! Fuck!"

The truck jerked back into my lane and I quickly veered over to my right, driving on top of the curb to avoid an accident!

"What the hell is wrong with ya'll?!" I screamed.

The truck slowly pulled back into their appropriate lane and I hesitantly pulled back onto the road. I instantly noticed the red light up ahead but I had no intentions whatsoever to stop. I didn't trust sitting at a red light with those idiots.

Pressing my foot down on the gas pedal, I quickly accelerated and sped through the red light, leaving the truck behind—

Beep!

"*Shit*!" I screamed after nearly colliding with a Dodge Caravan!

"Cameron?" Tiffany groaned. "Cameron, I don't feel so good. I think I'm gonna be sick."

"Come on, Tiff! You can't hold that shit in 'til we get home?" I asked clearly frustrated. I was still quite shaken up from the bullshit those guys had just pulled.

Tiffany ignored me as she opened up the back door and stuck her head out.

"Tiffany, what are you doing?!" I yelled.

There was no response, only the guttural moans of her emptying the contents of her stomach. She didn't even give me a chance to pull over.

Once she finished, she slammed the door shut and plopped back into her seat. "You gotta mint or something?" she asked.

***

The following morning, I had called a local mechanic shop to have my car towed from the hospital—luckily it wasn't already towed off the premises having been there overnight. Driving Jude's Fisker Karma, I decided to visit him today. I had to really get down to the bottom of this whole "Ericka thing" because I didn't know how far the bitch was planning on taking things in order to have Jude all to herself. I wasn't for the unnecessary drama.

I prayed Jude wouldn't have any visitors so that I could get some quality time with him, but to my dismay, I was met with the unexpected sight of Ericka sitting in the visitor's chair beside Jude's bed.

Before either one of them could notice my presence, I darted alongside the doorframe in order to eavesdrop on their conversation.

"She is the reason you're in here to begin with. Listen to yourself, Jude—"

"Every couple goes through shit, E," he argued. "I'm not finna leave my girl cuz that's what you want."

"Your mother hates her," Ericka continued. "In case you didn't know that."

"My mother ain't gotta date her," Jude joked.

"Jude," Ericka whined. "This is serious," she said. "I'm sure you know by now that I came back just for you. I want things to be the way they used to be. Remember those days?" Ericka reached over to touch Jude's cheek, but he quickly grabbed her hand in mid-reach. "Let me take care of you, Jude—"

"Look, E, I appreciate you comin' here. I'm diggin' the support. I really am. But real talk, shit ain't going down between us the way you want it to. And if you can't respect my relationship, then maybe you shouldn't come around anymore. I'm just saying."

Ericka looked offended as hell. "But—"

"Look, it ain't gone never be an us, E. Period. I'm not giving up on my girl, flat out—"

Ericka folded her arms. "Oh, you mean like how you gave up on me?" she spat.

Jude sighed in frustration. "Man, don't go there."

"Like you gave up on our future. You put the money in my hand and told me to get the abortion. Remember that?" Ericka's voice cracked as she spoke. "You gave up on me and our child. Why is this ghetto bitch so important to you? What the hell does she have that I don't? Huh?"

"Ericka, I'm not about to go there with you—"

"You know what? Fine! Alright, it's cool. Sooner or later, you'll start thinkin' with your head instead of your dick. And then you'll see what a big ass mistake you're making."

"Yeah, I hear you, E," Jude said nonchalantly.

Ericka snatched her purse off the plastic hospital nightstand and stormed out the room. She practically ran into me on her way out.

I couldn't help but to crack a smirk after she realized that I had been standing there all that time eavesdropping. "Obviously the better woman has won," I stated bluntly. I knew I was behaving childishly but I couldn't resist the urge to rub it in her face.

"Yeah whatever, bitch. You're just something to do for now. Believe that." She looked me up and down with disgust before walking past me, brushing against my shoulder slightly.

I watched Ericka disappear inside the elevator before walking into Jude's room.

"Hey, baby," I greeted sweetly.

"'Sup babe," he smiled.

I had planned on telling Jude about Ericka slashing my tires, however I realized now wasn't the time.

"So…um…I couldn't help but to overhear," I paused. "I didn't know you and Ericka's past was so deep—"

"Whatever you heard…that was me then…I wasn't ready to settle down. I was still a kid myself, you feel me?"

I walked over towards Jude and took a seat on the edge of his bed.

"I understand," I said.

Jude sat up in bed a little and motioned for me to come closer.

I eased up in bed and lied beside him. "Ericka is determined to get you back," I simply said.

"That chick hasn't been the same since the abortion."

I looked up at Jude in confusion. “What do you mean?”

“Well…she really wanted the baby to begin with. We went back and forth over the pregnancy for a while,” he explained. “By the time she went through with the abortion, she was five months.”

“Sheesh,” I commented. “I didn’t know they could do it that late into the pregnancy.”

“Yeah,” Jude sighed. “She was really fucked up afterward. Mentally…emotionally…And then six months later she lost her baby sister, Elise to leukemia…”

“Oh wow”. *Poor girl,* I thought. Suddenly, I felt sympathetic towards Ericka and understood her odd behavior a little bit more.

“She fell into a deep depression afterward. Started taking all types of pills and anti-depressants…” Jude looked out the hospital room’s window. “Shit got too real after she tried to commit suicide—”

“She tried to commit suicide?!” I asked in disbelief. *Oh hell no*, I thought.

“She overdosed on prescription pills,” he said. “Spent a little time in a mental facility…once she was released she enrolled herself in the Air Force. That was almost three years ago,” he explained. “We stayed in contact for the most part, talking to each other on the phone and shit…”

Smirking slightly, I asked, “Were you selling her dreams, Jude?”

“What do you mean?” he asked dumbfounded.

“You know damn well what I mean,” I said.

Jude shrugged. “I mean we *talked* about maybe getting back together and shit. But as time went on, I just lost interest in rekindling what we had.”

"In other words, you met Pure Seduction." I was being a smart ass now.

"Don't go there, bay," he warned me. "I mean, shit…we—"

"Sshh," I whispered before placing my finger against Jude's lips. "You don't even gotta talk about it anymore. That's the past," I told him. "We're the present and the future."

Jude smiled. "The future, huh?"

I slowly leaned over and kissed him.

"I like the sound of that," he said.

The sudden sound of someone clearing their throat interrupted our passionate kiss. Jude and I focused our attention on the nurse standing in the doorway.

"I hate to interrupt you two, but visiting hours will be ending soon."

"Okay," Jude and I said in unison. I turned to face my man. "Well, I guess I'd better get going." I gave him a peck on the lips. I also decided to withhold the fact about Jude's account being frozen. For now.

"Alright. Love you, babe," Jude told me.

"Love you too."

After giving him one last kiss, I made my way back to the car. I prayed Ericka hadn't slashed my damn tires again…or keyed the car for that matter. After everything Jude had told me about her, it was obvious that the chick had some serious problems, issues, and concerns. Honestly, I felt sorry for the girl.

Luckily, when I reached the car everything looked in order. I hit the automatic door unlock button—

"*Aye, bitch*?!"

I quickly turned around at the sound of the familiar voice—Suddenly Ericka launched a Burger King cup full of hot ass orange soda at me!

The beverage splattered all over my expensive Gucci drape dress. "*Oh, hell no*!" I screamed.

Ericka quickly skirted off in her Camry, but I was hot on her heels, as I hopped into my car and pulled off.

Chapter 9

I was in hot pursuit as I followed Ericka's silver Toyota Camry out the hospital's parking lot and into traffic. Ericka and I were pushing over forty miles per hour as we flew up Madison Avenue! We were in adjacent lanes shouting out threats and obscenities at one another through our lowered windows.

"Bitch, pull over!" I threatened.

"Kiss my ass!" Ericka retaliated as she accelerated ahead of me.

Her little Toyota Camry was no match against my sports car. I floored the gas pedal and we were once again side by side.

"Bitch, why don't you go back to whatever projects you came from?!" Ericka yelled.

"Hoe, I swear when I catch your ass—"

Screeeeeeecchh!

Boom!

My forehead instantly collided with the steering wheel! The impact was so hard that my car instantly launched backwards sending the Cadillac Escalade, I had just rear-ended, forward a few feet.

I was so caught up arguing with Ericka that I didn't even realize I was driving in a right turn only lane.

Ericka quickly sped through the yellow traffic light but not before tooting her horn twice as if mocking me.

Jude is going to freaking kill me, I thought.

I touched the center of my forehead where I quickly felt a speed knot beginning to form. My neck was sore from the instant whip lash, and I could taste blood in my mouth from when I had bit down on my tongue.

"Shit," I cursed surveying the damage from the inside of the car. The windshield was cracked. The driver and the passenger side windows were both shattered. "This is not happening," I said before trying to open up the driver door.

The driver of the Cadillac Escalade quickly hopped out his vehicle in order to survey the damage I had caused.

I instantly noticed the driver door wouldn't budge after the first few attempts but after ramming my shoulder against it a couple times, it finally pried open. Broken glass littered the street as I stepped out.

A red Honda Civic quickly pulled behind me and a white woman jumped out. "Oh my God! Are you alright?!" she asked in a concerned tone.

"I am *so* sorry," I expressed compassionately to the driver of the Escalade. His back was still turned to me as he looked over the damage I had caused. "I…I wasn't paying attention," I slowly made my way over towards him.

"What the fuck?!" he cursed. He would need a whole new frame, I assumed.

"I am so sorry," I repeated. "I have insurance. I—"

The guy turned around and faced me and my heart instantly sank into the pit of my stomach! My mouth was wide open as I stared into the dark, emotionless eyes of Pocahontas' killer!

"Kevin…" His name came out as an inaudible whisper.

When Kevin realized it was me who had rear-ended him, he looked just as surprised as I did.

Suddenly, I did the one and only thing I could think of at a moment like this. I quickly turned around ran off—however, Kevin unexpectedly grabbed my forearm before I was able to flee.

"*Let me go*!" I screamed. His grip was on my arm was firm. "Somebody help me!" My heart raced uncontrollably as fear coursed through my veins.

The crowd of onlookers quickly pulled out their cell phones, preparing to dial the police. Kevin probably thought I was crazy. After all, I was the one who had hit him, but I couldn't help the fact that I was scared as hell.

Flashbacks suddenly came to mind from when he had let loose two bullets into Pocahontas' body without so much as blinking an eye. I thought about how he stood over me as I laid in the middle of the street, with his gun aimed at me…

The moment I blinked I heard a single gunshot go off!

"Get off me!" I continued to yell.

"Yo, what the hell is wrong with you?!" Kevin yelled before releasing his grip.

I didn't stick around to answer as I hopped into the crashed up Fisker Karma—skidding the side of Kevin's truck as I frantically pulled off.

***

"What do you mean I need a police report?" I yelled into the receiver. I was on the phone with Jude's insurance company and they were giving me the runaround on the process of getting his car repaired.

"Yes ma'am. It's imperative that we have a police report. We also need to speak with the other person involved in the accident's car insurance company. Your settlement claim can take as long as two months—"

"Two months?!" I repeated. "I don't have two months."

"Well, ma'am, once you acquire the proper—"

I didn't give the customer service agent time to finish her sentence before I rudely disconnected the call.

"Jude is going to kill me," I told myself for the hundredth time. "Why the fuck did I just pull off like that?"

Tiffany was seated at the breakfast bar watching me practically throw a fit because of the dilemma I was in.

"Girl, you are acting like you can't scrape the money up to get his car repaired. You made six hundred last night and you told me that was a slow night. So how much are you raking in on a good night?" Tiffany asked. "Eleven…twelve hundred?" she said. "I don't even know why you're sweating it. Today's Friday. We'll make a killing tonight—"

"We?" I asked sarcastically.

Tiffany sat up in the bar stool and pushed her glasses up. "Yeah. Me and you. Who else?" she asked.

I snorted. "Girl, you are *not* going back to The Shakedown."

"What do you mean I'm not?" she asked.

"Tiff…," I sighed. "You ain't about that life, girl," I joked.

"What are you talking about? I did good last night." Tiffany sounded like a little child trying to convince their parents that they were now a big kid. "I did good," she stated again.

"Girl, good and drunk," I teased.

"I may have been drunk but I made pretty good money," she noted. "You can say what you want, but you're not about to stop me from shaking this ass."

I burst into laughter. "What ass?"

Tiffany tried to keep a straight face, but she quickly burst out laughing seconds later.

***

“Hold on,” Tiffany quickly spoke up. “Can you stop at that store? I wanna grab some gum real quick.”

I made a face. “Gum?”

Tiffany craned her neck to look at me. “Yeah. Gum. Can’t be up in no guys’ faces with funky breath,” she laughed.

“Girl, the club owner does not want us chewing no damn gum. He said it looks ghetto,” I told her.

Tiffany snickered. “Well, how the hell are we going to make sure we have minty breath?”

“Girl, you better pop a damn Altoid before you leave the dressing room. That’s what I do.”

“Well, pull over I need some mints,” she said.

Sighing dejectedly, I pulled my truck into the 7-Eleven parking lot straight ahead.

Tiffany hopped out the truck before me. “You want something from inside?” she offered.

“Nah, I’m coming in too,” I told her.

The minute we walked into the store, I went into the back and fetched a twenty ounce Pepsi from the beverage cooler. Making my way towards the checkout line, I suddenly felt someone grip my elbow. Yet, it wasn’t a firm or forceful grip.

His touch, however, felt very familiar. “Hey, what’s up, Cameron?” Klimaxxx greeted.

It had been quite a few months since we had last run into each other and sadly it was under unfortunate circumstances. Silk had been shot in the parking lot of Pandora’s Box after a brutal fist fight between him and Tank. Klimaxxx and I had rushed him to hospital that night; Silk was barely hanging on to an inch of his life. That was the last time we had seen one another.

"Hey. How have you been?" I asked.

Klimaxxx was dressed trendy wearing a Dolce and Gabbana Muhammad Ali t-shirt and a pair of gray cargo shorts. On his feet was the latest pair of Nike LeBron 9 shoes.

Klimaxxx was definitely an attractive guy. Standing at six feet two inches, he was dark-skinned with chiseled facial features. Full sleeve tattoos adorned both his arms and neck.

"I've been pretty good." He paused. "Aye, listen, I'm sorry about what happened—"

"It's fine," I waved him off. I really didn't want anyone else's sympathy because of Silk's death. I just wanted to move on with my life.

"Yeah, I didn't get a chance to make it to his funeral," he said. "I don't really do too well in settings like that. But I chopped it up for a minute at the Passover. I didn't see you there though," he acknowledged.

I tried my hardest to block the images out my head of Tamika kicking my ass mercilessly. "Yeah…uh…I left the service early," I simply said. He didn't have to know why.

"Oh, okay. Well, I ain't gon' hold you up, ma. But check this out. If you ever need anything, hit me up, aight? I could slide you my number…or you could give me yours," he said.

"Alright…I…damn," I muttered. "I done left my purse in the car…"

"It's all good. Shoot me your number real quick."

He pulled out his Samsung Galaxy S3 and I plugged my number in. "Alright, I'ma catch up with you," he said.

"Talk to you later, Klimaxxx."

He flashed a sexy smile. "Marcus," he said.

My eyebrows furrowed. "Marcus?"

He chuckled. "Yeah. That's my name. Marcus. That way you ain't gotta be callin' me Klimaxxx in public."

I nodded my head. "Ahh. Gotcha!"

"I'll hit you up," he said before leaving the store.

As soon as I made it to the checkout line, Tiffany wanted all the 411.

"Damn, who was that, Cam?" she asked watching him through the glass doors of the store. "He fine as hell."

I looked her up and down and smiled. "Hmm…let me find out you got a thing for male dancers."

Tiffany clamped a hand over her mouth and gasped. "Oh my God! He's a stripper?!" she yelled.

A few people in line turned around and scowled at us.

"Sshh," I whispered. "Yeah, he dances down at Pandora's Box."

Tiffany's eyes followed Marcus as he made his way over towards his royal blue Suzuki Hayabusa.

"Can I help you," the cashier interrupted whatever provocative thoughts Tiffany and I had going on in our minds.

After paying for our items, we made our way back out to the car. It wasn't until I turned the key in the ignition, that I suddenly realized Marcus aka Klimaxxx was the mysterious, masked dancer from Pandora's Box.

However, I decided to keep my thoughts to myself as we made our way to The Shakedown.

Chapter 10

I watched with a disapproving expression as Tiffany staggered towards the stage. It was barely midnight and the bitch had already managed to get herself pissy drunk once again! And if being inebriated wasn't bad enough, I could have sworn I saw a tiny glint of white powder underneath her nostrils under the fluorescent lighting of the club as she strutted across the stage.

I know this bitch wasn't back there in the dressing room snorting coke with Champagne's ass, I thought.

Figuring that it was best to holler at Tiffany about her "unusual antics" when we were all alone, I decided to work the floor until my turn on my stage. After Tiffany finished twirling around the pole—since it was obvious that she couldn't dance for shit, her turn finally ended and it was now my turn to go up.

Tiffany stumbled a little bit coming down the stairs from the stage and I had to grab her forearm to keep her from falling. "You good?" I asked her.

She held her head. "I just had too much to drink," she told me.

Now that I was a little closer to her, I could see the unmistakable white substance on her philtrum a lot more clearly. "Tiffany, what the fuck is that?" I asked knowing very well what it was. "Bitch, I know you weren't back there sniffing that shit!"

"Next we got coming to the stage, a sexy ass tenderoni that goes by the name of *Hypnotic*!" DJ Chaos announced my entrance on stage, making it clear that I needed to get my ass up there and do my thing.

Tiffany swiftly wiped away the residue. "I—"

“Alright now fellas! Show my girl some love! If you ain’t got no more singles, I suggest you hit up the bar and re-up on some bills!” DJ Chaos yelled into the microphone.

“I gotta go up on stage. Meet me in the back when I get done. I wanna holla at you,” I told her in a serious tone.

Tiffany looked down at the floor like a child being scolded by their parent.

I rolled my eyes before sashaying up the stairs. My turn on stage couldn’t have gone by any faster and once my two songs ended, I hurried down and made my way to the dressing room—even ignoring a few guys who wanted a bit of one on one attention. I wasn’t thinking about any of them though, I had a mouthful to say to Tiffany.

Drinking was one thing but this chick had taken it to the next level. I knew this lifestyle was new to her, but she was obviously taking the path to self-destruction. In a way, it was entirely my fault. I should have never introduced her to this stripping shit knowing her goody goody ass would never be able to handle it. This was obviously not a life she was fit for.

Even though I knew I would miss out on some serious money to be made tonight, I planned on paying the club owner, Ahmad, the tip out fee and taking Tiffany’s ass home. Not my home either. She could get all her things from my house but then she had to go!

The minute I pushed open the dressing room door, I was met with the unexpected sight of Tiffany being confronted by Champagne. A group of dancers stood around, eagerly anticipating for some action to pop off.

“Bitch, I know you took my shit!” Champagne was standing but a mere few feet away from Tiffany. She was also shoeless and obviously ready to brawl if need be.

Tiffany was leaning against the lockers looking as lost as I felt at this exact moment.

“I don’t know what you’re talking about,” Tiffany said in a non-confrontational tone.

“Look, ain’t nobody shit ever came up missing until you got here, new girl,” Vixen cut in. “So if you stole Champagne’s shit just admit it.”

Chyna stood beside Vixen with her arms folded across her breasts, ready to jump in any fight her sister got in. The last thing Tiffany wanted was to be jumped on by the two of them. I had heard the stories about how the two of them had jumped some chick in the strip club a few years ago and cut her face up pretty bad with a piece of glass. Talk about heartless.

“I’m telling the truth,” Tiffany cried. “I didn’t—”

“Look, hoe, either you gon’ gimme the money I paid for it, or square the fuck up! Plain and simple.” Champagne clapped her hands together to add emphasis. She was now giving Tiffany an ultimatum.

“She’s giving you a choice!” Chyna cut in.

“I’m not about to fight,” Tiffany said modestly.

“Fuck that!” Champagne yelled before throwing a vicious punch that landed right in Tiffany’s face!

Tiffany’s head bounced off the locker and her hands instantly went up to protect her face. It was obvious that my girl was no fighter.

“Hold up!” I yelled. “Hold up, ya’ll! *Chill*!” I quickly made my way over towards the fight.

Champagne had a fistful of Tiffany’s micro braids locked in her grip as she pummeled her skull with her free hand.

“You gon’ steal from me, hoe?!” Champagne yelled.

Tiffany tumbled to the floor but before she could get to her feet, Champagne kicked her in the side.

"You fuckin' bitch!" Champagne screamed.

Tiffany tried her hardest to stand back up but to no avail, she fell right back onto the dirty floor. Evidently, she was not used to wearing the six inch heels she had to dance in.

"Champagne, man, chill!" I yelled, trying to help Tiffany stand up.

Vixen gave me a gentle shove. "Naw, Hypnotic! Let 'em fight!"

"At least let her take her shoes off!" Juicy yelled.

I ignored all the dancers who were obviously enjoying the fight. I tried to step in between the two but Champagne was determined to kick Tiffany's ass over the stolen drugs.

"Move, Hypnotic!" Champagne screamed trying to get around me. "This ain't got shit to do with you. This between me and ya sheisty ass girl!"

"It ain't worth fighting!" I yelled.

"This dirty bitch stole from me! It's the mothafuckin' principle!" Champagne hollered with her fists still clenched.

Tiffany struggled to get to her feet. Individual micro braids littered the dressing room floor from when her hair had been snatched out. "I didn't take your stuff—"

"Bitch, shut that shit up! You saw where I stashed my shit yesterday after you did a line with me!" Champagne yelled.

So there it was, I thought. I turned around and looked at Tiffany in disbelief. The good girl I had always known her to be no longer existed. Although, I was mad as hell at her, I couldn't stand to see her getting her ass mopped all over the dressing room floor.

"Tiffany, go tip out and meet me in the car," I told her.

Tiffany quickly grabbed her belongings and rushed for the door.

"You saved that hoe this time, Hypnotic, but it ain't over! Believe that," Champagne warned me. "It ain't fuckin' over."

***

"Dude, what the hell is wrong with you?" I lashed out at Tiffany the minute I climbed into the truck.

"She just straight attacked me for no reason!" Tiffany cried wiping her tears away with her wrist.

I gave Tiffany a skeptical look. "One thing about these hoes, they aren't just gonna fuck with you for no reason, Tiff."

Tiffany's mouth fell open. "So you don't believe me?! I didn't take—"

"Tiffany, I saw the shit all up under your nose when you were on stage! Why are you lying?! You don't have to lie to me," I told her. "I'm not them. I'm your friend, remember? You can keep it a hundred with me."

Tiffany sighed dejectedly. "I don't even wanna talk about this," she huffed before taking it upon herself to turn the music on.

MGK's "Est 4 Life" blared through the speakers of my car.

I am from the city where they—blaow—love that gun sound!

I quickly turned the music off. "Tiff, when we get back to my house, I want you to get your stuff together and then you gotta go."

Tiffany whipped her head in my direction. "What?!"

"I'm sorry, girl. But you gotta go—"

"Cameron, please! Look, I'm sorry! I fucked up today! I don't know what's gotten into me—"

"I don't know what's gotten into you either," I cut her off. "I can't believe you, Tiff. What the hell would possess you to stick some shit up your nose?" I doubted this was her first time using.

"It was just…I just…," she hesitated. "I just wanted to try it. I've been so depressed about finding work and everything…I just figured if I did it, it would take the stress away, Cam—"

"And taking Champagne's shit?!" I added.

"I honestly don't know what possessed me to do that," she admitted.

"Tiffany, you can't just be starting trouble and expecting not to have to pay the consequences. You're stealing and shit…and you want me to be cool with letting you stay in my house—"

Tiffany quickly turned to face me. "Cameron, please! I fucked up today. It won't happen again. I swear on everything I love, I would never *ever* steal from you. You're my girl!"

"Tiff, you gotta go—"

"But I can help you pay the mortgage for the condo. I can give you money to help get Jude's car fixed. Admit it," she said. "You need help. With Jude's account being frozen you're going to need all the financial help you can get."

Tiffany had quickly managed to turn the tables. As much as I wanted to tell her about herself, she was undoubtedly right. I *did* need all the help I could get financially.

Before I could even open my mouth to respond, the sudden tapping at my driver window interrupted me.

I turned my head to see who it was—I only caught a glimpse of the metal bat that came crashing through my driver's window only seconds later!

Tiffany screamed at the exact same moment that the glass shattered! I instantly turned my head in order to keep glass from flying into eyes.

"You bitch! You don't listen!" Ericka screamed before taking a vicious swing at my driver door.

Tiffany was screaming at the top of her lungs in the passenger seat as Ericka continued to assault my truck with her bat.

I knew the bitch was nuts from everything Jude had said, but I had no idea she was this damn crazy!

"What did I tell you, bitch?!" Ericka screamed. "*Huh*?!"

Bow!

Ericka knocked the side view mirror clean off!

"I told you to stay away from him!"

I tried to open the driver door but Ericka took a vicious swing at me—I quickly slammed the door shut before she could knock my head off with the metal bat.

"Who the hell is she?!" Tiffany screamed, cowering in the seat beside me.

"Put the bat down, hoe!" I screamed.

I ignored Tiffany as I tried to step out of the car again. This bitch had life all the way fucked up, tearing my brand new truck up. If she wanted to act crazy, I could act crazy right along with her ass.

"*Why won't you just go the fuck away*?!" Ericka screamed.

I quickly jumped out of the truck in an attempt to rush Ericka before she swung the bat again—surprisingly, she was a lot faster than I had imagined. She took a swing at my head, but I quickly raised my left arm, blocking the blow. The bat collided with my forearm but I was so pissed that my brain didn't even register the pain right away.

Before she could swing again, I ran up on her and grabbed the bat.

Ericka and I were in the middle of the street, outside of The Shakedown wrestling to get the bat from one another.

After several seconds of wrestling and tussling with each other, I finally managed to snatch the bat from Ericka's crazy ass. Before she could react, I sent a forceful kick that connected with her midsection.

She dropped to the pavement instantly, cradling her stomach.

"I'm sick of your ass, bitch!" I screamed before raising the bat—

"Cameron! *No*!"

Tiffany grabbed the bat before it came crashing down onto Ericka's skull. She was curled up into a ball, fearful of the vicious beating that she knew was coming.

"She's not worth it," Tiffany said in a calm tone.

I allowed her to slowly take the bat from me. Looking around I noticed that a small crowd had formed in front of the club. Funny, how no one but Tiffany had bothered to stop me from beating Ericka's skull in. There were even a few guys with their cell phones out recording the entire scene.

"Man, I'ma put this shit on World Star!" one of the guys proclaimed.

"What the hell ya'll just standing around lookin' for?!" I screamed.

"Come on, Cameron," Tiffany urged. "Let's just go home."

I took one look at my truck and nearly burst into tears. I could've snatched the bat from Tiffany and beat Ericka's ass to a bloody pulp.

"*Fuck*!" I screamed.

The sudden sound of laughter behind me instantly stopped me in my tracks. I slowly turned around and watched Ericka pick herself up from the ground.

"I'm not gonna stop, bitch!" Ericka laughed sadistically. "I'm gonna keep fucking with you until your stupid ass gets the point," she said. "I can do this shit all day, Cameron. It's just a matter of how much *you* are willing to tolerate before you finally give in. I'm willing to do whatever it takes to get my man," she told me. "How much are you willing to take to keep him?"

"You fuckin' bitch!" I screamed, running towards her—but Tiffany quickly grabbed me from behind.

"She's not worth it, Cam," Tiffany said.

Ericka smirked at me as she firmly stood her ground.

I spit in her direction even though my saliva was nowhere near close to reaching her.

Tiffany forced me to turn around and walks towards my dented up truck to avoid any further altercations.

"Let the police handle it," Tiffany told me.

At the sudden mention of police, Ericka quickly came to what little senses she had left. Without deliberation, she high-tailed it towards her Camry parked on the opposite side of the street.

Tiffany pulled her cell phone out and attempted to snap a picture of Ericka's license plate.

Ericka quickly pulled off and fled up St. Clair Avenue.

"Shit," Tiffany cursed walking back over towards me. "The damn numbers came out blurry—"

I waved her off. "It's okay. Let's just go home."

"Are you sure, Cameron because—"

"It's cool," I answered in an irritated tone. "Let's just go."

I felt a total combination of embarrassment and hatred as I climbed into my battered Audi truck and prepared for the long drive home.

Chapter 11

The following morning, I dropped the Audi truck off in the same shop that was currently working on repairing Jude's car. Needless to say, the mechanics were more than surprised to see me twice in the same week with yet *another* fucked up car.

Tiffany was right about one thing. If it wasn't for bad luck, I wouldn't have any at all. Luckily for me, the mechanics agreed to a payment plan and I was able to pay for the repairs in installments.

Ericka was costing me money with her foolishness and I didn't know how much more of her bullshit I could take. Not to mention, she had fucked my arm pretty bad when she hit me with the bat last night. My entire forearm was sore and tender to the touch. I feared I might have even had a sprained arm messing around with her crazy ass.

I doubted I would be shaking any damn thing tonight with a sore arm. Unfortunately, I would be missing out on some potential money tonight. Once I made it back to the condo, I was surprised to see that Tiffany was not there—considering I had her car. After checking my cell phone for any missed text messages or calls, I noticed that I had received a text message from her saying she went to kick it with some guy she had met at The Shakedown last night.

I shook my head in disbelief after reading the message. I should have had a talk with her about that shit but she was grown after all and she was free to do whatever she wanted as long as she didn't bring any niggas up in here.

It actually felt good to be alone though. I finally had some peace of mind to think and reflect on all the crazy shit that had taken place in less than a month's span. I had to talk to Jude and tell him everything, including his funds and his crazy ass ex-girlfriend's antics last night.

Scrolling through my contacts, I suddenly came across my father's sister's name. I had yet to call my Aunt Linda, but I couldn't deny the fact that I felt a little awkward. Raised in orphanages and foster homes, I was never able to establish that familial bond with anyone including my own relatives.

Sighing dejectedly, I locked my phone and tossed it on the bed a few inches from me…only to retrieve it two minutes later.

"What the hell?" I asked myself before dialing Linda's number.

After the fourth ring I figured she had to be at work. Just as I was about to disconnect the call, her raspy voice filled the receiver.

"Hello?"

"Hey…um…"I cleared my throat. "This is Cameron. You told me to...um…"

"Hey, Cameron! I was wondering when you were going to call me," she said cheerfully. "What are you up to?"

"Oh, nothing actually. I was just…"

"Nothing? Well why don't you come over?" Linda asked. "I can make us lunch and we can talk and catch up with one another."

"Um…well…," I hesitated. "Alright," I finally agreed. What the hell, it wasn't like I was doing much of anything else today and I did still have Tiffany's car.

After rattling off her address, I took a quick shower and dressed. Linda stayed off Madison Avenue, so it wouldn't take too long to get to her house.

Fifteen minutes later, I pulled into the driveway of a quaint, little yellow brick home. After killing the engine, I made my way to the front porch. Linda opened the door for me before I could even knock and pulled me into a bear hug like we'd been close all my life. After awkwardly returning her affection, she led me inside.

"Don't you look cute," she complimented taking in my appearance.

I was dressed casually today wearing a floral halter sundress and brown gladiator sandals.

"Thank you," I said.

"You must get your keen fashion sense from this side of the family," Linda beamed.

I slowly took in her attire from head to toe. She wore a powder blue wool sweater—even though it was damn near ninety degrees outside—and a pair of chocolate flare corduroys.

Ha! I think not, is what I wanted to say, but instead I replied, "You never know, Aunt Linda. I probably did."

"Well, don't just stand there. Come and have a seat," she beckoned for me to follow her into her small den.

I took a seat on the aqua colored loveseat and she sat in the matching reclining chair adjacent to me.

"How old are you now?" she asked.

I twiddled my fingers nervously. "Um…nineteen. I'll be twenty in a couple weeks." It felt so weird to me sitting here talking to an aunt I didn't even know had existed until a few days ago.

Linda covered her mouth with her plump hand. "Oh my goodness. You're still a baby, Cameron," she said. "I thought you would've been a little older. How old is your brother now?" she asked.

My eyebrows furrowed. "What?" I laughed. "Brother? I don't have a brother," I told her.

Linda looked just as confused as I felt right now.

"What do you mean you don't have a brother…what's his name…? Um…" She began snapping her fingers as she tried to recall the name of my nonexistent brother.

"Uh…my mother didn't have a son," I politely spoke up. "Just me. I'm an only child," I explained.

Linda smiled and waved me off. "Yeah, I know you are Barbara's only child but Kenny had a son—"

"My father?!" I asked in disbelief. This woman didn't know what the hell she was talking about. I was my father's only child…or so I thought.

"Yes." Linda nodded. "You have a half-brother. Kenny had a child with a woman he met during his stint in the military. This was before he even met your mother." Linda stared at me in confusion. "Cameron, I can't believe you didn't know this."

My mouth was slightly agape as I digested everything that Linda had just said.

"You're telling me I've had a brother out here all this time and I never knew it?" I asked in disbelief. "I think you're mistaking me for someone else—"

"Cameron, I don't know what reason your father had for not telling you this. Maybe he felt you were too young to understand then. You were just a kid…Maybe Barbara might have not wanted you to know. I'm not sure. But as sure as the sky is blue, I'm telling you, Kenny has a son," she said. "You have a brother."

I shook my head still in disbelief. "No this…this isn't…no…" I was in denial.

Linda quickly stood to her feet. "Wait a minute. I think I have a picture of him and his mother. It might be a few years old. Kenny gave—"

"My brother?" I asked incredulously. "Does he know about me?"

Linda's expression was one of utter pity. "I assumed you both knew of each other. I've never spoken to him a day in my life so I can't say if he knows about you or not. Your father gave me the picture about a year or so before he died," she explained. "But what I don't understand is why Kenny never told you all this himself."

"Maybe he was planning to but then he got killed…"

There was suddenly an awkward silence between us. We avoided eye contact for a minute before Linda spoke again.

After clearing her throat, she said, "I'm going to see if I can find that picture."

"Alright," I muttered.

I still didn't fully believe Linda. All my life I had believed I was an only child and then here she came, out of nowhere, telling me that I had a half-brother out here somewhere that probably didn't even know I existed. This shit couldn't be happening.

Linda quietly left the room as she went to retrieve the picture of my so-called brother. Suddenly, my cell phone rang. After checking the caller ID, I noticed Jude was calling me from his hospital room.

"What's up, babe?" I answered exasperatedly.

"What's up, boo?" he asked. "You sound a lil' aggravated."

"No…um…," I cleared my throat. "I'm all good. What's up with you?" I asked. "How are you feeling today?"

"A little sore but they gave me some medication for it. I'm calling to let you know that I'm on my way to therapy."

"Really?" I asked. "Aww, I want to see you before you go in. You're on your way there right now?"

"As soon as the nurse gets here, yeah."

I quickly stood to my feet. "I'm on my way up there now," I told him before quickly disconnecting the call. "Um…*Aunt Linda*?" I called out.

"Yes?!" she hollered from a nearby room.

"I actually gotta get going," I told her. "I gotta go take care of something. It's important."

"Oh…well…okay. Just lock the bottom lock behind you."

"Alright, it was nice talking to you," I told her.

"I'll let you know when I find the picture. Okay?"

"Okay," I replied halfheartedly. Apart of me still didn't or couldn't believe I had a brother. I still thought she didn't know what the hell she was talking about.

After leaving Linda's house, I sped to the Cleveland Clinic in order to see Jude before he went off to therapy…unfortunately when I made it up to his room he wasn't even there. A passing nurse saw me standing in his room and informed me that he had already left for therapy. Chalking my visit up as a loss, I decided to go on back home.

When I made it back to the car, I was shocked to find Tiffany's car wouldn't even start up. The gas needle read that the tank was half full so I didn't know what was going on. The engine turned over a few times but it wouldn't start up.

"What the fuck?!" I cursed aloud.

After trying to start the car up a few more times, I decided to call Tiffany. Unfortunately, I was sent straight to her voicemail.

"Ain't this a bitch?" I asked myself. There were no buses that I could catch that would take me back to my condo and it would cost a grip catching the taxi. Realizing that my options were limited, I figured I would go ahead and call the cab.

I barely pressed a digit before my phone suddenly began ringing the set ring tone, “Cashin’ Out”.

I didn’t recognize the unfamiliar number but I decided to answer anyway. “Hello?”

“Hey, what’s up?” A deep voice filled the receiver.

I didn’t recognize the voice right away. “Hey, who’s this?” I asked.

“Marcus.”

My eyebrows furrowed. “Marcus?” I asked in confusion.

“Klimaxxx,” he simply said.

“Ohhh. Okay. I have to get used to calling you Marcus,” I told him. “But anyway, look, now’s really not a good time—”

“Everything good?” Marcus asked in a concerned tone.

“Yeah…well…no,” I hesitated. “I’m actually stranded up here at the Cleveland Clinic in Lakewood.”

“Word? I could come swoop you up if you need me to,” he offered.

“Thank you,” I said. “I would really appreciate it.”

“Aight. Gimme about fifteen minutes, ma.”

Chapter 12

My arms were folded across my chest and my expression was one of pure disdain. *Hell no*, I thought.

Marcus pulled alongside me on his Suzuki Hayabusa bumping French Montana's "Everything's A Go". I had forgotten just that quick that he rode a bike when I actually expected him to pull up in a car. Nevertheless, he did look kind of cute in a blue and white varsity jacket, a pair of khaki short and the latest Jordans.

Don't do that, Cameron, you got a man, I told myself.

"I've never gotten on a motorcycle before," I told Marcus after he pulled off the royal blue helmet.

"For real?" Marcus laughed. "You good. I promise you ain't got nothin' to worry about, ma," Marcus said. He handed me the helmet. "I wouldn't let nothin' happen to you. Come on."

I unfolded my arms and stared at the Suzuki Hayabusa for several more seconds. Swallowing my fear, I reluctantly made my way over towards the bike and straddled it before pulling the helmet over my head. Slipping my arms around his waist, I held on tight for dear life much like I had the night he had spun me around on stage.

I would be lying to myself if I said his toned midsection didn't feel good holding on to. *Stop it Cam, you got a man*, I chastised myself for the second time.

"Alright, just hold on tight," Marcus said. "Don't be nervous."

Marcus revved the motorcycle up, and my grip around his waist instantly tightened.

He peeled out the driveway and zoomed up Madison Avenue, swerving in and out of lanes. My sundress ruffled in the wind.

This isn't so bad, I thought.

"You good?!´Marcus shouted over his shoulder.

"Yeah!" I hollered.

Marcus increased speed as he flew up the street. He even took a few shortcuts in order to get to my house quicker. Ten minutes later he pulled right in front of my condo and killed the engine to his bike. He helped me climb off the bike and I quickly patted my sundress in place.

"Let me get that for you," he offered, carefully removing the helmet from my head.

"Thank you," I told him before finger combing through my bob.

"No problem," he said. "What you finna get into?"

"Nothing. Nothing at all."

"You ain't workin' today?" he asked me.

Marcus knew that I was an exotic dancer. He just didn't know that I was supposed to have been a retired one. "No. I actually sprained my arm at work," I lied.

"Damn. That sucks," he said. "So what you got planned for today?"

"Shit. Nothing. I'll probably just chill all day," I told him.

He chuckled. "On a Saturday, Cameron?" he asked. "It's too nice to be sitting in the house all day. Why don't you let me take me take you to get a bite to eat or something," he offered.

Turn around and go into the house was what my conscience was telling me to do but instead I blurted out, “Um…sure.”

Without hesitation, I climbed back onto the bike and pulled the helmet over my head.

***

“You ever been here before?” Marcus asked once we were seated at a table.

“No,” I answered. “But I heard this place being advertised on the radio.”

Marcus and I were at the Luxe Kitchen and Lounge on the west side of Cleveland. There was a pretty decent crowd inside during lunch time.

“I hit this spot up on the regular sometimes. It’s straight,” he said. “I’m surprised you haven’t been here though.”

“This is a pretty nice restaurant,” I said admiring the scenery.

“You’re pretty,” Marcus suddenly admitted.

I looked over at Marcus seated across the table from me. *I know he is not hitting on me*, I thought. Needless to say, I felt a tad bit awkward. Yes, Marcus was definitely sexy and he seemed like a great guy but I couldn’t see myself talking to him because he was once cool with Silk.

Besides that, I had already talked to two male dancers. I didn’t plan on dating anymore in the near future. And thirdly, I already had a damn man, I reminded myself for the third and final time.

Marcus gazed at me for a few seconds before he cracked a smirk and shook his head.

"What?" I smiled.

"Man, that day I pulled you on stage…I was thinkin' to myself, 'please don't let this dude come out here and see me dancin' on his chick'. I saw firsthand how crazy that nigga used to act over you—not that I can blame him though."

I began nervously fidgeting with the bundled utensil set. "Yeah…Silk would've been mad if he came out and saw me on stage with you," I muttered.

Marcus chuckled. "He would've been even madder if he knew I was diggin' you ever since I first saw you."

I cleared my throat and looked away apprehensively.

"My bad," he quickly said. "I shouldn't have said that knowing everything you've been through lately." He hesitated. "So um…you wanna get a drink or something while we're waitin'?"

"Alright." Indeed, I could use one. Marcus had definitely created some tension after letting me know that he was feeling me.

I followed Marcus to the bar where we placed our orders. I decided to keep it light and ordered a raspberry Bomb Pop. Marcus ordered a Corona. The minute I turned around to head back to our table, I nearly collided with a female who was damn near standing right behind me. I accidentally sloshed my drink on her lace tunic.

"Oh, my bad—Tiff?! Girl, what are you doing here?" I asked surprised to see her at the exact same spot as me.

Tiffany wiped away the splattered beverage on her shirt. "Girl, I told you I was going out to kick it with my new lil' friend," she smiled.

My gaze then traveled to the tall, chubby guy standing beside her—my mouth instantly fell open. The wine glass slipped from my fingers and crashed into the carpeted floor, shattering upon impact.

Wallace stood proudly beside Tiffany with a stupid ass smirk pasted to his face. My jaw hardened and my nostrils flared at the very sight of him. The images were forever painted clearly in my mind from when Wallace had brutally raped me several months ago. I was still emotionally scarred from that night and just the sight of his ass made me sick.

Why the fuck is he here with Tiffany, I thought.

"I got it," Wallace spoke up reaching down to pick up the broken glass.

"No, I got it," I quickly said.

Wallace and I reached down at the same time. His hand brushed against mine as we both went to retrieve the same piece of glass. Suddenly, I just snapped! "I said I got it! Get the fuck away from me!" I yelled, tempted to stab his ass with a shard of glass if he got any closer.

"Damn, Cameron," Tiffany said in disbelief. "What the hell is up with you?" she asked.

Wallace and I both stood to our feet, never breaking gazes with each other.

He even had the nerve to smirk. "Yeah, what I do?" he asked mockingly.

"Nigga, you know what you did," I answered through gritted teeth.

Tiffany looked over at Wallace in confusion.

Wallace sucked his teeth and waved me off. "Bitch, ain't nobody do shit to yo' ass," he said. He was obviously still in denial about what he'd done to me that night. Evidently, he didn't understand the difference between rape and consensual sex.

Marcus quickly stepped in. “Aye, my dude. Ain’t no need for all that,” he told him.

Wallace looked Marcus up and down in disgust. “Nigga, fuck you!” he spat.

“Fuck me?” Marcus suddenly shoved Wallace. “Fuck you!”

As expected, Wallace didn’t back down from an altercation. He shoved Marcus back, and Marcus retaliated by shoving Wallace even harder and further.

Wallace accidentally fell into a passing guy and his friend. They both grabbed Wallace before he could get at Marcus again.

“Get off me!” Wallace yelled thrashing in the two white men’s embrace. “Bitch nigga, I’ll see yo’ punk ass out here!” Wallace threatened.

Marcus held his arms out. “It’s whatever, my nigga!”

“Marcus? Marcus?!” I spoke up.

He quickly turned to face me and I let him know that I was ready to leave right now.

“Man, alright,” he answered in an irritated tone.

I didn’t even look in Tiffany’s direction as Marcus and I headed towards the exit door.

Chapter 13

"My fault about all that shit at the Luxe," Marcus apologized after I climbed off his bike. "I just been fuckin' up all tonight, huh?" he asked. "I hope I ain't ruin any chances I had with you."

I handed him his helmet. "Actually…um…there is no chance with me, Marcus," I informed him.

He raised an eyebrow in skepticism. "Word?" he asked in a defeated tone.

"Yeah. I gotta dude," I admitted.

Marcus sucked his teeth and sighed for good measure. "Damn."

I turned and headed towards my front door.

"I don't believe you," he suddenly said.

I turned back around and faced him. "What?" I asked confused.

"I don't believe you," he repeated. "About me not having a chance with you," he said. "I think I do. I just think they're slimmer now."

My lips formed into a slight smirk. "I wouldn't get your hopes up," I told him. "I love my man."

Marcus smirked. "No shade, but I'm finna change that shit, ma."

***

Twenty minutes after I made it in the house, Tiffany came strutting through the front door. I immediately went in on her ass.

"Where the hell did you meet Wallace? And why weren't you answering your phone earlier."

This bitch had the nerve to roll her eyes at me. "In case you haven't noticed, I'm a grown ass woman, Cameron," she retorted. "And I met him at The Shakedown. I told you already. Remember?"

"You told me you met some guy. I didn't know it was him! Look, Tiffany," I approached her. "That dude is 106othing' but trouble. Trust me." I was too embarrassed to even speak about the rape.

"Like I said I'm grown," she retaliated. "I can take care of myself, Cameron."

I folded my arms and stared at her in disbelief. "Well, why are you living here in my house? Eating my food? And sleepin' in my damn bed, Tiffany?" I asked her. "Answer me that. You really think you know that nigga? Well, let his ass take care of you. And speaking of him, I know you didn't let that nigga know where I lived."

"He picked me up and dropped me off," she answered. "How was I—"

"Tiffany, you brought him here?!" I screamed. "Are you fuckin' kiddin' me?!"

"What is up with you and him?" Tiffany asked me. "What? Ya'll used to fuck with each other or something?"

"Tiff, stop fuckin' with that dude, aight? He's bad news," I told her. "Just promise me you'll leave him alone, aight?"

"Okay, alright," she quickly said in order to shut me up.

"I'm serious," I stressed.

"I am too. Look," she quickly fished in her purse and retrieved her cell phone. "I'm deleting his number right now," she said. "Better?"

"Yeah. I feel a lil' better," I answered.

"Good. Now where's my car?"

"Yeah about that…it wouldn't start up. It's in the hospital parking lot. I don't know what happened. The gas needle was on the halfway point—"

"Oh, girl, I forgot to tell you, I got a floater. That damn needle doesn't work. It probably ran out of gas." Tiffany walked over to the breakfast counter and plopped down. "We'll go get it tomorrow. Anyway enough about that. What's up with you and Mr. Exotic Dancer?" she asked.

"Who? Marcus?" I said it like it was no big deal. "There's nothing up with us? He picked me up after your ratchet car broke down and then took me out to get something to eat...and then all that other shit happened," I added. "He dropped me off and I made sure to let him know that I had a dude."

Tiffany twirled a braid around between her slender fingers. "Yeah you'd better tell his ass. Or else I'm telling Jude."

"Girl, bye. It ain't nothing going down between us."

Tiffany twisted her mouth up. "Yeah…you sayin' that now…"

***

I was at the bar giving a guy a lap dance when I noticed Champagne walk past and mean mug the hell out of Tiffany. She was too busy fishing in the guy's pocket that she was giving a lap dance to, to even notice.

Shaking my head in disapproval, I couldn't believe this bitch had only been dancing with me for two weeks and already she was pickpocketing. Naturally, I thought about Pocahontas and how her greed had ultimately led to her demise. This bitch was going about the hustle all wrong, I thought.

Tiffany finished her lap dance before me and I watched as she made her way to the locker room, probably to stash the guy's wallet she had just stolen. My gaze then drifted over to the guy who didn't even realized he had just been robbed blind.

The tall, heavy set guy stood up, rubbed his hard on through his True Religion jeans, and then took a swig of his Budweiser. I watched as he walked towards the foot of the stage where Juicy had shimmied up the bronze pole and made her ass clap in midair.

I figured he would reach in his pocket and retrieve his money, but he simply nodded his head in approval before swaggering out of the club with his bottle still in his hand.

I let out a sigh of relief. If he would have noticed his wallet was missing right then and there he would have known automatically that Tiffany had just swiped his shit.

"Thanks, sexy," my customer said once the song finished. He placed a fifty dollar bill in my garter belt. After thanking him, I made my way to the dressing room to confront Tiffany about the slick shit she had just pulled.

I found her sitting at the vanity beside Juicy, toking on a blunt. *When she started smoking*, I thought.

"Temptation, lemme holla at you for a minute," I said in a stern tone.

Tiffany burst into a fit of coughs. "What's up?" she asked in between spasms.

I looked from Juicy to Tiffany. "Meet me in the bathroom," I said before leaving the dressing room.

Two minutes later, Tiffany pushed open the wooden bathroom door. The restroom had only one stall but it still managed to serve as a second dressing room to most dancers.

"What's up, girl?" Tiffany asked looking in the cracked bathroom mirror at her reflection. She tucked a few loose braids behind her ear.

"I saw what you just did out there," I told her.

"What?" she asked dumbfounded.

I propped my hands on my hips. "Don't play dumb. I saw you pickpocket the nigga you was just giving a lap dance."

Tiffany waved me off. "Psssh! Oh that? Girl, I been doing that shit for a minute now."

"Tiffany, did you forget how Pocahontas got her ass bodied?"

Tiffany snorted. "Well that was her ass. She obviously was too messy with it. I'm a smart bitch. These niggas be so into getting their lil' dicks grinded on that they don't even be feelin' me slippin' my fingers into their pockets," she bragged. "I swear it's as easy as takin' candy from a damn baby. You should try it, Cam—"

"Girl, bye. You talkin' crazy," I told her.

"What?" she asked offended. "It's not like I'm makin' as much money as you and Juicy and 'em. I gotta do a lil' extra to make ends meet…"

I threw my hands up in mock surrender. "You know what? That's on you, Tiffany," I said. "You startin' to feel yourself a lil' too much. Don't ever say I didn't try to warn you."

***

After tipping out, Tiffany and I made our way towards the exit. I was feeling a little better because I had met my quota for the night and then some. The mortgage would be paid in full and I could toss some money to my mechanic for the repairs. I was feeling good after tonight's fruitful endeavor.

"Alright, Damon! Alright, Ahmad! See ya'll tomorrow!" I waved goodbye.

"Where the hell are my car keys?" Tiffany complained fishing through her purse. "Oh, here. I got 'em." She opened the door and I followed her outside. "You know what we should do tom—"

Whap!

Tiffany was suddenly struck in the face with the hard, steel butt of a Glock 17! Tiffany instantly dropped onto the pavement. It had all happened so quickly that it took my brain a few seconds to register what was going on.

We're about to get robbed, was the first thought that came to mind.

"You lil' thieving ass bitch! I ain't that nigga! Where my money at before I put somethin' hot in ya ass!" The guy who Tiffany had robbed earlier was standing over her with his gun aimed and finger resting on the trigger.

Tiffany wiped away the thick blood oozing from both her nostrils. She then spit out a mouthful of blood onto the ground. One of her front teeth rested in the center of the pool of dark red blood.

"Please don't kill me," she cried. "I didn't take your money."

"Bitch, do it look I'm playin'?!" he spat. "You was the only fuckin' hoe I got a lap dance from. Don't fuck with me!"

“Leave her alone!” I suddenly found my voice.

The guy instantly aimed his gun in my direction. “Don’t be a captain-save-a-hoe. This ain’t got shit to do with yo’ ass.” He then re-aimed his weapon towards Tiffany who was still lying on the ground. “Where’s my shit?!”

“I…I don’t know what you’re talking about…”

He suddenly stepped on Tiffany’s fingers; the sole of his Timberland boot crushed her fingers.

“Tiffany, just give him his shit!” I screamed.

“*Ow*! *Ow*! Okay! Okay!” Tiffany screamed. “Please stop!” Blood trickled from her mouth as she plead with him to release her fingers.

I was scared shitless and I didn’t know what the hell to do. I just knew I didn’t want to die over a few dollars.

Hesitantly, he lifted his foot off her hand and allowed her to retrieve his money.

With trembling fingers, Tiffany quickly fetched the guy’s wallet from her duffel bag and handed it to him.

He quickly snatched the thick wallet and walked off towards his purple old school car as though he had not done anything wrong.

Juicy suddenly walked out the front door and was met with the unexpected sight of Tiffany lying on the ground with a bloodied face.

“What the hell just happened?”

I let out the breath I’d seemingly been holding ever since I stepped foot outside.

“That guy just robbed me,” Tiffany cried.

Chapter 14

It was crazy how Tiffany always seemed to manage to get herself into trouble no matter what. In all actuality, she was just another Pocahontas. Always getting herself in some shit and then dragging me along for the ride.

After taking her to the hospital, I decided to have yet another talk with her about giving up this stripping shit.

"Cameron, I'm not gonna stop because of what happened tonight," she surprisingly said.

"Tiff, you just got your fuckin' teeth knocked out of your mouth tryin' to scheme—"

"Well, I've got thirty-one left," she retorted.

We were sitting at a red light at the intersection of 22nd street and Carnegie Avenue. I turned to my girl. "Tiffany…you're my friend," I told her. "I care about you. You ain't got shit to prove to me—"

"I know I don't," she said. "And real talk, this isn't even about you. It's about me," she told me. "I like dancing."

"What about you getting that that job?" I reminded her.

"Fuck that job," she said. "I'm making way more doing this then I ever would working a nine to five."

I looked at her in disbelief. I almost didn't recognize my friend from the way she was talking right now. "What the hell is happening to you, Tiff?" I asked her. "This isn't you. Remember how you used to scold me about what I did? You used to encourage me to want to do better for myself. What happened to that Tiffany?"

Tiffany rolled her eyes and looked out the passenger window. "That Tiffany is dead…"

Before I could open my mouth to respond, a car suddenly beeped its horn behind me, signaling that the light had turned green. For the remainder of the ride home, I didn't say a word. It wasn't until I pulled Tiffany's Nissan Altima into the garage that I decided to speak again.

"Tiffany, as your friend, I'm telling you that I don't think you should go back to The Shakedown. I saw what this lifestyle did to Pocahontas…trust me you don't want that ending."

Tiffany looked over at me and grimaced. "Like I told you before, I can take care of myself." With that said, she hopped out the car and slammed the door behind her.

I sighed out of frustration before I climbed out the car.

***

The loud and annoying sound of my "Cashin' Out" ringtone woke me up the following morning. Groaning, I reached over for my cell phone on the nightstand but accidentally knocked it onto the carpet.

"Ugh," I moaned in irritation before reaching over to pick it up.

It was 8:16 a.m. and the caller ID indicated that it was my Aunt Linda. "What does she want?" I asked. "Hello," I answered in a muffled tone.

"Hey! Good morning, Cameron!" Linda greeted cheerfully. Obviously, she was a morning person. "I'm calling to let you know I found the picture!"

"Hey, Aunt Linda," I greeted exasperatedly. "I was actually still asl—"

"What are you doing right now?" she cut me off. "I'm off today. You should come over. I made homemade blueberry muffins."

My stomach growled at the very mention of blueberry muffins. With all the shit that was going on lately, I hadn't been eating much at all.

I pulled the covers off me and sat up in bed. "Alright. Give me an hour."

"See you then."

I disconnected the call and went into the master bathroom to freshen up. I had butterflies in my tummy and I was nervous as hell. I figured it was because she had found the picture of my "so-called brother." What if she was right? What if I really did have a brother that I knew nothing about?

So many thoughts ran through my mind as I showered. Did he know about me? Where did he live? How old was he? If my father met his mother during his brief period in the military, my brother could be living anywhere in the country and not necessarily in Ohio.

After I threw on some clothes, I made my way towards Tiffany's room. The door was closed but I figured she was awake because I heard soft music playing from the opposite side of the door.

I started to just give her space but my nosiness eventually got the best of me. As quietly as I could, I cracked open the door an inch or so and peered into her bedroom.

Tiffany stood in front of the dresser, looking at herself in the mirror as she cried softly.

What the fuck is up with her, I thought. I figured she must have been upset about what happened last night.

As her friend, I knew it was my job to console her while she dealt with whatever problems she was currently faced with but I didn't know what to say in her case. She was so hot and cold, I didn't want to accidentally offend her. Especially considering how sensitive and defensive she could be. Against my better judgment, I closed the door and gave her space to wallow in her own sorrows.

After grabbing Tiffany's keys off the counter, I sent her a text message letting her know that I was taking her car for a little while. I made it to my aunt's home in fifteen minutes tops. The front door was already open for me, but she didn't greet me at the door like she had done last time.

"Hello?" I called out before knocking on the screen door.

"Yeah! I'm in here, Cameron," she hollered. "Come in!"

I stepped inside and found her in the kitchen stirring a pot of oatmeal on the electric stove.

"Hello. How are you?" I asked her.

"Doing pretty good. You eat oatmeal?" she offered.

"Oh no," I laughed. "I ate a lot as a kid," I told her. As a matter of fact, we ate it damn near every morning in the orphanages.

"The muffins are on the counter. Help yourself." She turned the fire off. "I'll be right back. Let me go and get this picture."

"Okay. Is it alright if I use your bathroom?" I asked.

"Sure. First door in the hallway on your left."

After using the bathroom, I made my way back into the kitchen. She still had to return so I decided to go ahead and help myself to a blueberry muffin. I took a seat at the kitchen table. I was halfway done with the muffin when she returned with a faded Polaroid picture.

"Found it last night," she told me. "Here you go. You can have it."

I wiped the crumbs off my hand using my jeans and took the dated photo from her—the half-eaten muffin instantly fell out my hand and onto the wooden table. My eye shot wide open at the sight of the teenage boy standing beside his mother. He was dressed in a cap and gown and it was obvious this was his graduation picture. Although the picture was old, his face was unmistakable!

This cannot be my fucking brother!

Scribbled in faded blue ink across the white strip, at the bottom of the photo, was my brother's name and the year the picture was dated. It also said 'From: Kenny To: Linda' beneath the date.

No! No! No! *This is not happening*!

"Are you alright, Cameron?" Aunt Linda asked in a concerned tone.

Suddenly, vomit shot up my throat—I quickly dropped the photo and took off running towards the bathroom.

"Cameron?!" Linda called out.

Barely making it to the toilet, I flipped the seat up and emptied the contents of my stomach into the porcelain bowl.

Aunt Linda suddenly appeared in the doorway. "Are you okay?" she asked.

I couldn't speak as my body jerked from the painful stomach spasms. Seconds later, more vomit shot up my throat and into the toilet.

"You aren't pregnant, are you?" Linda asked in a low tone.

Pregnant?

With all that was going on, I had not once took that into consideration. Nor did I notice that my period was weeks late.

"Shit," I whispered to myself.

Chapter 15

I felt like I had just saw a ghost as I took a seat on the edge of my bed. An unopened EPT pregnancy test sat on my left side as I stared off into space. I was mentally fucked up after finding out who my long lost brother was. On top of that, I was only moments away from discovering if I was pregnant or not.

Picking up the framed portrait of me and Jude at Colby Park, I looked over the picture. Tears suddenly slipped from my eyes as I became emotional. *If I am pregnant, I can't have this damn baby*, I told myself. I didn't know the first thing about being a mother. Hell, I had only known mine for eight years of my life before she was killed.

"God, please…please don't let this test come back positive," I prayed. Fall semester was beginning in a month and I was not trying to juggle school and a baby. "Please don't let me be pregnant," I whispered.

The mattress creaked as I stood to my feet. Grabbing the pregnancy test off the bed, I slowly made my way into the master bathroom.

***

I tapped lightly on the door before slowly making my way into Jude's hospital room.

He stopped flicking through channels long enough to look in my direction. "There's my girl," he smiled.

"You're looking and sounding a lot better," I noted.

"Feeling a lot better too," he added.

I made my way over towards his bed and gave him a peck on the lips. "I'm sorry I didn't get a chance to see you before therapy."

"You ain't gotta apologize. I'm just happy you here, bay. How're you feeling?" he asked.

I let out a sigh of frustration. "I've uh…it's been a lot going on, Jude," I admitted.

He sat up in the hospital bed and turned to face me. "How so? Talk to me, bay."

"Well…" I paused. I couldn't even find the words to say it. I didn't even want to hear myself say it. Instead, I reached into my purse and pulled out the used pregnancy test. Without a word, I handed him the results.

"What's this?" he whispered, taking it.

"I've taken two this morning," I told him. "…They both came back positive…"

Jude looked up at me in astonishment. He opened his mouth and then closed it quickly as if he didn't quite know what to say. "This…I'm going to be a dad," he finally said. "Why are you looking and sounding so sad, bay? This is great news!" he beamed.

Tears filled my eyes and I swallowed the large lump that had formed in my throat. "Jude, we can't afford to have any kids right now…"

"What?" he asked. "What do you mean?"

The next thing I pulled out of my purse was the letter from the IRS. "I'm sorry I went through your mail," I said before handing him the piece of paper.

Jude silently took the letter from me and quickly looked it over. "*What the fuck*?!" he yelled in anger.

A few passing nurses looked into the room but thought better to mind their own business.

"They froze my fuckin' accounts?!" Jude tossed the letter and it fell onto the tiled floor. "Come the fuck on, man! This ain't happening!"

"Just try to relax," I said in a soothing tone.

"Relax?" he looked at me in shock. "What the hell you mean relax? I'm flat ass broke! I'm finna go to jail! You're fuckin' pregnant. How is the mortgage going to get paid? How are the bills going to be paid?!"

"I've been working," I finally admitted.

He paused. "What do you mean you've been working?"

"I've been dancing—"

"You've been stripping while carrying my damn baby?!" he lashed out.

"I just found out this morning, Jude," I answered defensively. "Relax. It's not like I'm showing anyway. And besides," I added. "I haven't put much thought into keeping the baby…"

If Jude would've whipped his head in my direction any harder, he might've snapped his neck. "What the hell did you just say?" he asked in a low tone. "You're thinking about getting an abortion? Are you crazy, Cameron? You're not killing my fucking baby."

"Well, you sure didn't hesitate to have Ericka's baby aborted." The minute it slipped from my lips, I instantly regretted saying it.

There was an uncomfortable silence between the two of us before Jude spoke again.

“Wow, Cameron.” He shook his head. “You don’t cease to amaze me lately,” he said. “I done told you that I wasn’t ready then—”

“And what makes you think you’re ready now?” I asked. “I mean, you said it best. We’re broke and you’re supposedly on your way to jail. You expect me to be a fuckin’ single mom?”

“I damn sure don’t expect you to be up on stage shakin’ your ass while carrying my child!”

I couldn’t even talk to Jude anymore. There was too much going on already and right now I just wanted to get away from him. I quickly stood up and headed towards the door.

“I’m not having this damn baby, Jude,” I said before leaving the room.

***

“Hey girl!” Tiffany beamed the minute I entered the house. It was like she hadn’t even suffered a major breakdown only hours ago.

“Wow. Someone’s rather chipper,” I said sarcastically.

She laughed. “A little. Well anyway, I’ve been thinking. We work hard right?”

I plopped down into a bar stool at the breakfast counter. “True.”

“Why don’t we say fuck The Shakedown tonight and go kick it in the Flatts? We ain’t been down there since our freshman year. Remember those days,” she smiled.

I would have to get used to seeing that missing tooth in the center of her mouth. “Yeah, I remember those days,” I answered.

“Remember the time when you got so hammered off those Long Island Ice tea’s that you threw up on the dance floor,” she laughed.

“Oh, come on, Tiffany. Don’t remind me.” I was growing nauseated just thinking about it.

“You think that sexy ass Chinese security guard still works down at Earth Night Club?” she asked. “Remember I used to have the biggest crush on him!”

I laughed and shook my head. “Girl, I don’t know.”

“So what’s up? You tryin’ to kick it tonight or what? You been so stressed out about this and that. At least take a night to enjoy yourself, you feel me? I mean, for God’s sake, girl, you’re only nineteen. And you haven’t said a word about what you’re planning for your birthday.”

I instantly clapped my palm against my forehead. “Shit, I forgot. My birthday *is* in a couple weeks!”

“See!” Tiffany wagged her finger at me. “You’re doing too much, Cameron. It’s time to relieve some of that stress and enjoy yourself,” she said. “Starting tonight. We’re club hoppin’ down in the Flatts today!” she said excitedly.

Tiffany was so determined to kick it that I didn’t have the heart to turn her down even though I wasn’t really on it. Right about now, I wanted nothing more than to curl up in my bed and cry. I didn’t plan on telling her about the pregnancy. I still had a hard enough time grasping it myself.

Chapter 16

French Montana's "Pop That" was bumping through the speakers inside of Earth Night Club. Downtown Cleveland was popping on this particular Saturday night. The clubbed was so packed that we barely could make our way to the center of the dance floor through the massive crowd of people.

Tiffany was hyped as hell tonight. She hadn't had a drink yet and she was behaving like she had drunk four Red Bulls. When we made it to the center of the dance floor, she immediately went ham.

She wore a short black dress that had a split down the center, revealing what little cleavage she had to showcase. Although the dress barely stopped an inch above her ass cheeks, that didn't stop her from bending over and popping her ass all buck and wild on the dance floor.

It was crazy how Tiffany had managed to transform so quickly. The once shy and timid goody goody girl was indeed gone.

"What's up sexy? You trying to dance?" A ball head guy made his way behind me anticipating a little 'twerk-action'.

"Nah, I'm good," I told him. Hell, I got paid to dance on niggas. Why the hell would I want to dance for free? I wasn't trying to be stuck up. I was only keeping it real.

"Bitch," he muttered before walking off.

"Whew! Cameron, girl! I am having too much, fun!" Tiffany yelled in excitement.

We were barely on the dance floor for five minutes and she was already pouring with sweat.

"Oh my God!" she suddenly proclaimed. "Look over at the bar! Look! It's your boo!"

I quickly turned in the direction of the bar anticipating to see Jude, but instead I saw Marcus standing with a couple of his homies looking right in our direction!

I rolled my eyes and looked back at Tiffany. "Girl, that is not my fucking boo," I told her.

"Say what you want, Cam, but he already put his foot in the door when you let him take you out to get something to eat."

"That's all it was!" I argued.

She pursed her lips. "Try telling that to Jude—Ooh, girl! Look at him! Look at him! He's looking right at you!"

Hesitantly, I looked over in Marcus' direction.

"Look at the way he's smiling," Tiffany said. "It's like he's saying 'Watch me work'! Girl, he's finna turn your world upside down!"

"Pssh! Bye!" I waved her off before turning away from him.

"Oh my goodness! He's coming over here right now!" Tiffany yelled excitedly. "I guess I'd better make myself scarce. I'll be at the bar—"

"No, Tiff! Don't leave…"

My sentence trailed off as Tiffany quickly left me stranded in the center of the club.

"Wow. You look nice," A familiar voice whispered in my ear from behind. The hairs on the back of my neck instantly stood up.

I wore a BeBe red and gold armor dress and a pair of gold floral encrusted sandals. A gold bangle set the outfit off. I knew I was killing it tonight. I always made it my sole mission to step out dressed to impress.

"I know," I said boldly without turning around to face him.

"I see you over here brushing niggas off," he said. "Probably givin' them the same ole tired ass 'I got a man speech'," he teased. "So what's up? I know you gon' let me dance with you." His confidence was on full display tonight.

My gaze wandered over towards the bar where I saw Tiffany flirting with a guy in the wheelchair who frequented The Shakedown from time to time. Focusing my attention back to Marcus, I asked, "If I told everyone else no, what makes you think I'm gonna say yes to you?"

"I danced for you," he laughed. "Hell, you owe me a dance for real."

I couldn't help but laugh at his response before finally turning around to face him. "I don't owe you anything," I said sarcastically.

He nodded his head. "You're right. But it'd be nice if you returned the favor."

I caught a generous whiff of his Clive Christian cologne. Marcus looked fly as hell in a V-neck Gucci t-shirt and a pair of crisp dark denim jeans. On his feet was a pair of Gucci Canvas high-top sneakers.

Kirko Bangz "Drank in my Cup" suddenly began playing throughout the club.

"Come on, Cameron. Dance with me. This is my shit," he said, gently pulling me closer to him.

I looked over in Tiffany's direction once more. She was now sitting in the lap of the guy in the wheelchair, smiling and flirting away while nursing a Blue MF.

I focused my attention back to Marcus. For a brief moment, I allowed all my problems to be pushed to the back of my mind. My brother. The bills. The pregnancy.

Marcus slipped his arms around my waist and we danced to the mellow beat of Kirko Bangz's single.

Girl, I know how much you really want somebody…

We were both so in tune with each other that it felt like we were the only two people on the dance floor—Suddenly, a white flash snapped me from my profound thoughts! Obviously, I wasn't the only one who noticed the strange light as Marcus looked around in puzzlement.

"The fuck was that?" he asked.

"I don't know," I said looking around as well. "Looked like someone just took a picture though, didn't it?" The club's photography center was located in the back of the club so I knew the flash couldn't have from that.

"Yeah. That was weird," he said. "Maybe someone nearby was snapping photos."

I then looked over in Tiffany's direction—however she was no longer there. She and the guy in the wheelchair were both gone!

Don't panic, I told myself. They could be anywhere. After all, there was a VIP room upstairs. Pulling my cell phone out of my clutch, I quickly dialed Tiffany's number in order to see where she had gone. The last thing we needed was to be split up in this big ass club. However, to my dismay, there was no answer.

"You good?" Marcus asked noticing my uneasiness.

"I don't see my girl at the bar," I told him.

"It's cool. Just chill. She's probably around here somewhere. This is a big club. You want me to help you look for her?" he offered.

"I'd appreciate it," I told him grateful for his assistance.

"I'll go look outside real quick," Marcus said. "You never know, she might have gone out for a smoke."

"Alright, I'll check the VIP."

"Meet me back at the bar, alright?"

"Cool," I agreed.

He made his way outside to look for Tiffany and I went upstairs in search of my girl. I didn't find her in the VIP room or in the pool table area for that matter. I even checked the women's restroom.

"Where the hell did this bitch go?" I asked myself.

Ten minutes later, Marcus met me at the bar as promised. "I didn't see her outside," he informed me.

"I didn't even see the nigga in the wheelchair she was talking to," I told him. "Hold on a second." I pulled my cell phone out and called her twice. "No answer," I said before disconnecting the call. "I know this trick did not just leave me here!"

Marcus rubbed my upper arm. "Chill, ma. I got you if you need a ride home," he offered.

"Good. Because I'm ready to go now," I answered in an irritated tone.

"Alright then. Let me go tell my niggas I'm finna bounce. I'll be right back."

With folded arms, I made my way to the exit. I couldn't believe Tiffany's ass had just up and bounced. When I made it outside, I didn't see her car parked across the street, confirming that she truly had left.

"Wait until this bitch gets home," I told myself.

I suddenly felt a hand softly touch the small of my back. "I was looking for you, baby girl. You ready?" Marcus asked.

I nodded my head and followed him to a black 2012 Chrysler 300. “Where’s your bike?” I asked after he hit the automatic door unlock button.

We climbed into the car at the same time. “At the crib. I rented this just to stunt in for tonight,” he laughed. “You like it?” he asked.

I shrugged. “It’s aight?” I answered sarcastically.

“Aye, at least I ain’t gotta worry about it breaking down on me,” he teased.

“Shut up,” I laughed.

Marcus turned the on CD player and Future’s “Turn on the Lights” played through the Beats Audio system.

He shifted the gears into drive and merged into traffic. During the silent drive home, I felt Marcus looking over at me from his seat a few times. Looking out the passenger window, I pretended that I didn’t notice his constant gazes.

Marcus suddenly turned the music down. “So…um…this is the second time I came through for you,” he said. “Where ole’ dude be at? ‘Cause I’m starting to think you ain’t really gotta man and you just givin’ me the runaround.”

I turned to face him. “I do have a man, Marcus,” I said defiantly.

He snorted. “Every time I wanna blow down, you *always* got a man,” he said. “I was patient with you to leave Silk’s ass but I don’t think I got much patience left. I’m finna steal your ass from this ‘so-called’ nigga you got.”

“I told you don’t get your hopes. I love my dude.”

“I’m gonna make you love me,” he said.

I turned to face him and smiled. “You are so cocky. It’s not even funny.”

“I’m not cocky. I’m confident,” he corrected me. “And when I want something, I’m determined to get it. This is a real nigga right here.”

I sighed. “All men say that.”

“I ain’t all men,” he argued.

“They say that too,” I added.

He chuckled. “You and this ‘imaginary boyfriend’. And what’s up with ole girl?” he asked. “Leaving you at the club and shit? You be surrounding yourself with a lot of people that ain’t shit.”

I sighed dejectedly. “Tell me about it.”

Fifteen minutes later, Marcus pulled in front of my condo. He shifted the gears into Park and sat there as if expecting something.

“Thank you,” I quickly said before opening the passenger door.

“Hol’ up real quick. What’s up?” he asked. “Are you gonna let me take you out again since that busta ruined our night?”

I hesitated. “I…um—”

“Oh yeah…that’s right…yo’ nigga. I forgot,” he said in a mocking tone. “I guess I’ll see you around then. Tell that nigga watch his back too,” he laughed.

I climbed out the car. “I’ll tell him,” I said before closing the door.

***

An hour after I made it into the house, Tiffany came strutting through the front door as though she had done nothing wrong.

I immediately went in on her ass. "Where the hell have you been? And why the fuck did you leave me at the club?!"

Tiffany tossed her purse on the end table in the foyer and smiled. "Relax, Cameron. Damn, I knew you were in good hands," she said knowingly. "Shit, I saw your ass on the dance floor practically giving Marcus a lap dance standing up," she laughed.

I, however, didn't see a damn thing funny. "You didn't answer my question," I said. "Where the hell did you go?"

"I followed the nigga in the wheelchair to the Marriott down at Key Center." Tiffany burst out laughing. "Girl, I fucked the shit out of that paraplegic ass nigga!" she bragged. "And it was good as fuck…well for me it was," she boasted. "Too bad his ass couldn't feel shit. Anyway, he paid me two stacks, girl! Easy money, just like that!" she snapped her fingers. "Hell, the dick was so good, I should've been paying him!" she laughed.

I didn't say a word as I shook my head. "I don't even know who the fuck you are," I finally said. I turned and walked to my bedroom.

"Come on, Cameron. Don't be like that!" Tiffany called out after me.

I slammed the bedroom door behind me.

***

The following afternoon I was able to pick my Audi truck up from the shop. The car looked the same as it had the day Jude pulled up on me at the Cleveland State dorms and told me it was mine. Not a scratch, knick, or dent on it. Jude's car wouldn't be ready until next week but at least I didn't have to drive Tiffany's Nissan any longer.

My Aunt Linda called me as I was leaving the mechanic shop but I didn't answer. Truthfully, I didn't want to be bothered. After discovering who my brother was, I just wanted a little bit of space.

When I finally made it back home, I was surprised to find Tiffany gone yet again. It didn't matter to me though. I didn't feel like looking at her face anyway. I was still mad at her ass for leaving me at the club.

The minute I walked into the house, I was greeted with a funky smell from the kitchen. "Damn, trash," I mumbled.

Damn, I miss Jude, I thought as I pulled the trash bag from the container. After tying up the Hefty bag, I walked across the parking lot the dumpsters and tossed the trash bag inside.

As I made my way back across the parking lot towards my condo, I thought about Ericka and how I had not seen or heard from her in a few weeks. *Maybe she finally decided to back the hell off*, I thought.

Fishing the house keys out of my pocket, I proceeded to unlock the front door—The unexpected feeling of someone rushing me from behind caused me to drop my keys! My entire body was roughly pressed against the front door after my unknown aggressor pinned me down.

"What do you want?!" I screamed in fear. "Please! Get off me! I can't breathe!" I squealed.

"Miss me?" A familiar deep voice whispered in my ear.

Chapter 17

My lungs were crushed against the front door as my aggressor pinned his body against mine.

"You should already know," he said. "Some pussy. Why the fuck is you playing?"

"Please," I choked out. "I…I can't breath—"

"Get your keys out and open the mothafuckin' door!"

Tears streamed from my eyes. "I can't move," I cried.

My aggressor roughly turned me around to face him.

The minute I saw who it was, I began crying even harder. "You're just going to do this to me right here? In the broad daylight?" I cried.

Wallace gritted his teeth like a mad man. "Aye, you should know by now that I don't give a fuck."

Tiffany's simpleminded ass had led him straight to me. *I am going to kill her*, I promised myself.

"Please don't do this," I pleaded. "You don't have to do this again." Snot trickled from both my nostrils. "I'm…I'm pregnant," I cried.

He laughed heartlessly. "Bitch, what the fuck that got to do with me?"

Click!

Wallace and I both focused on our attention to the loaded gun that had just been cocked. Jude stood a few feet from us as he aimed his gun at the back of Wallace's head. Defeated, Wallace had no choice but to release me and I wasted no time as I ran to my man.

Wallace snorted and shook his head. “This nigga,” he laughed.

“Yeah, mothafucka. This nigga,” Jude said still aiming his gun at Wallace.

“Please don’t shoot him!” I quickly spoke up.

“Why?” Jude asked. “Why shouldn’t I put something hot in this nigga for putting his hands on you?”

I briefly hesitated. “He’s not worth it,” I told Jude. “Just put the gun down.”

“Yeah, listen to yo’ bitch!” Wallace said with a taunting grin pasted to his face.

That comment really pissed Jude off. His grip around his gun instantly tightened. “Nigga, what?!” His finger was so close to pulling the trigger.

“*Jude, no*! He’s not worth it. Fuck him! Just put the gun down,” I advised him. “Think about our baby,” I added as a last effort.

Jude’s expression softened a little. Reluctantly, he lowered the weapon.

Wallace smirked and slowly walked past us. “Fuck nigga,” he spat.

“Let me catch ya ass over here again, I won’t hesitate to bust on sight,” Jude threatened.

“I ain’t worried about it,” Wallace said as he walked off.

“I’m going to file a report,” I said. “But for now please just come in the house before any neighbors see us…if they haven’t already,” I added.

Jude hesitantly followed me into the house.

“They released you today?” I asked. “I thought they were keeping you for a couple of months for observation.”

“I discharged myself today,” he simply said. “I had Tez come and pick me up. I can’t afford to be sittin’ up in no damn hospital and having my pregnant girl strippin’ and shit. I gotta make some moves,” he said. “You and the baby gotta have something—”

“What about your therapy? I don’t think you should’ve discharged yourself. And what do you mean you gotta make moves?” I asked.

Jude walked round me and into the master bedroom. I was hot on his heels, of course.

“What do you mean you gotta make moves?” I repeated.

“Meaning I gotta do what I gotta do, bay,” he said. “I can’t have you out here struggling with my baby,” he said. “Fuck that. It’s slow out here for that shit,” he said. “And I wasn’t diggin’ that abortion bull you was talkin’ the other day either. You don’t just make decisions like that on your own, Cameron.”

Jude proceeded to slowly undress.

“Did they give you something for your back pain?” I asked concerned.

He took a seat on the edge of the bed and removed his Jordans. “Yeah, they did. I’m straight,” he answered in a stubborn tone.

I came over and joined him in bed. “I still think you should’ve stayed in the hospital,” I said eyeing the surgical scar that ran vertically down his back.

“I told you, Cameron. I can’t afford to be sittin’ up in the damn hospital any longer. I got moves to make. Shit, we gotta eat right? I’m not finna have my baby moms out here fucked up when I’m gone.”

I scooted closer to Jude and placed my arm over him torso. "Why do you always say that? When you're gone? Or when you're locked up?" I asked. "There isn't a guarantee you're going to jail."

Jude ran a hand through his loose dreadlocks. "Bay…," he chuckled. "I ain't got a lawyer. I can't *afford* a lawyer—"

"What about the lawyer you used for assault charges? You said he was pretty cool. You don't think he would do pro-bono?"

"He's cool, Cameron. But that doesn't mean he don't talk money. Like you said, everybody has to face their consequences someday. And when I do I just want to make sure you and the baby are straight."

I sighed dejectedly. "Jude, are you sure you're ready for this?" I asked. "This is a big step," I paused. "Not just for me, but for you too. We don't know the first thing about being parents."

"I'm sure when you graduated high school and went to college you didn't know everything—if anything at all…but you learned right? And so will we. Have a little faith," he brought my hand to his lips and kissed the back of it.

"And what about us when—if you end up going to jail?"

Jude looked at me in confusion. "What do you mean what will happen to us?" he asked. "Baby, I thought the day we moved in with each that I had solidified myself in your life. What you got doubts for now?" he asked. "We gon' ride with each other no matter what happens. You feel me?"

"Yeah. I hear you."

"Come here. Give me a kiss."

I leaned closer and brushed my mouth over his soft lips. He groaned inwardly as he slipped his tongue inside my mouth.

"You know I missed the hell out of you, right?" he whispered. "I missed all this," he squeezed my ass gently. "Hell, I even miss the taste of you."

I smiled. “Well, why don’t you refresh your memory,” I teased.

“Say no more,” he said before positioning himself at waist level.

I lifted up a little in order for him to ease my jeans down my legs. After removing them, he tossed them onto the floor. Not bothering to take my thong off, he simply moved the silk material to side.

“Oohh,” I moaned after his mouth closed over my pussy. My back arched as his tongue flickered over my throbbing clit.

The sensation between my thighs felt so good that I actually found myself easing away. Jude quickly locked his arms around my thighs and firmly held me in place. His tongue dipped in and out of my walls.

Soft moans and whimpers reverberated off the bedroom walls as he devoured my pussy. I grabbed a handful of his dreadlocks and encased my bottom lip. “Ooohh, that feels good, baby,” I moaned. My breathing got heavy as I prepared for the approaching orgasm. “Mmm…baby,” I panted. “I’m about to cum.” My entire body tightened up as a tingling sensation shot throughout my entire body before settling at the tips of my toes.

Jude climbed alongside me and pulled me into his arms. Seconds later, slumber engulfed me.

***

The mattress creaked as Jude slowly climbed out of bed. Through a cracked eyelid, I watched as he grabbed his cell phone off the nightstand and tiptoed out the bedroom.

What the hell is he up to, I asked myself.

I knew I should've minded my own business, but against my better judgment, I pulled the sheets off me and quietly climbed out of bed. Peering out the cracked bedroom door, I watched as he stepped out onto the living room patio.

I felt like James Bond in 007 as I quietly crept out the bedroom and ducked out of sight in order for me to eavesdrop on his conversation.

"Yo, what's up man? Yeah…about what we talked about earlier…I'm still down if you tryin' to do that tonight. Shit, fa sho'. Cam is pregnant. My fuckin' bank accounts been frozen. Shit's real out here, nigga. So what's good? You sure the nigga gon' be at the spot? Okay, cool cool." Jude chuckled. "This mothafucka finna be in for a rude awakening. Aight, I'll get up with you later on."

I quickly darted back into the bedroom before Jude could see me. I hurriedly climbed into the bed and pulled the sheets over me. Jude entered the bedroom seconds later and joined me in bed. He slipped his arm around my waist and held me close.

I stared off into space, with my back turned towards him, wondering what the hell he was planning on getting himself into.

Chapter 18

"Where are you on your way to?" I asked as I watched Jude dress. It was going on damn near 10:00 p.m.

"Oh, me and Tez finna go down to Scorchers. Shoot some pool. Have a couple drinks, you know," he said nonchalantly. "That's cool with you?" he asked.

I pulled the sheet around my bosom. "Yeah. It's cool," I answered halfheartedly. I knew he was shooting me some bullshit but I decided not confront him for now.

He pulled a black Nike hoodie over his head. "Oh, yeah. Where's the Karma?" he asked. "I ain't see it in the garage."

My heart rate instantly sped up. "I um…I put it in the shop to get some minor work done to it. Nothing too serious. It'll be all ready for you in a couple days," I smiled sweetly.

Jude gave me a skeptical look. "Aight. So you gon' let me push the truck…unless you got somewhere you tryin' to go?"

I reached into the drawer of the nightstand and tossed Jude the keys to the Audi truck. "It's all yours," I told him. After pulling a Raider's snapback low over his head, he gave me a kiss on the forehead. "I might be out late, aight? Don't wait up for me, baby."

"Alright, sweetie. Be careful."

"You know I will," he said before leaving. "Lock the door behind me."

The minute I heard the front door close, I quickly jumped out the bed and hurriedly threw on some sweat pants and a t-shirt.

Grabbing Tiffany's car keys, I rushed outside. Jude had just pulled out the parking lot when I climbed into Tiffany's Nissan Altima. I started the car up and pulled out the parking lot making sure to say several feet behind him.

It was perfect though because he had no idea what Tiffany's car looked like, so he probably wouldn't even notice me tailing him. Nevertheless, I tried to keep a car in between us as I followed him to his secret destination. And it damn sure wasn't Scorchers which was located in Warrensville, Ohio. Actually, Jude wasn't driving anywhere near the city of Warrensville.

Instead, Jude led me straight to the east side of Cleveland. Fifteen minutes later, he made a left down 146th street off Harvard Avenue. He pulled alongside the curb and parked his car across the street from a brick house. I stayed a few feet behind him and killed the front lights to my car. Seconds later, his cousin Tez walked through the screen door carrying a duffel bag. He, like Jude was dressed in black from head to toe.

"What the fuck are they about to get into?" I asked myself.

Tez swaggered across the street and climbed into the passenger seat. They sat in the car for about ten minutes, obviously plotting on something big. When Jude finally did pull off so did I.

I followed him through the side streets before we ended up on Kinsman Avenue. Ten minutes later, he pulled into the Garden Valley housing projects located on 79th street.

"This damn sure ain't Scorchers," I said to myself.

I pulled into an empty parking space but decided to keep the engine running. Taking in my surroundings, I wondered what the hell Jude was doing over here, and what he had planned—Suddenly, I noticed a familiar face standing outside one of the units.

Kevin was posted on the steps in front of an apartment with a couple of his homies. They were drinking, smoking and chopping it up. I assumed this was where he lived but I wasn't sure. After all, I knew he had money. Surely, he could afford to stay somewhere nicer than some remodeled housing projects.

I suddenly thought about Pocahontas and how she had preferred to live in the hood even though she made enough money to live in a nicer area. She was always boasting about how comfortable she was living in the hood. I assumed Kevin felt the same way.

Snapping myself from my thoughts, I focused my attention back to Jude's car—I quickly noticed that neither Jude nor Tez were in the car any longer. Looking around the parking lot, I instantly spotted the two of them. They were couched down, creeping alongside a few cars as they made their way towards Kevin and his crew—while carrying sub machine guns! Black bandanas were tied around their faces and their hoodies were pulled extra low over their heads.

Some shit was definitely about to pop off!

"What the fuck should I do?" I asked myself panicking. And what beef did Jude have with Kevin?

Before I could decide what the hell to do, the sudden sound of yelling and shouting caught my attention!

"*Get on the ground*!" Jude yelled. "Get on the mothafuckin' ground!"

Kevin and his homies instantly dropped onto the pavement and placed their hands on the back of their heads.

"Empty ya fuckin pockets!" Tez shouted. "Money, wallets, jewelry! All that shit! Throw it on the ground!"

"Fuck that!" Jude yelled. "Where's the mothafuckin' stash at, nigga?!" he aimed his sub machine gun at Kevin.

"Fuck you, nigga!" Kevin spat! "You ain't gettin' shit from me, dog!"

Evidently, that was the wrong choice of words. Jude quickly snatched the black bandana off his face to show just how serious he was. "Nigga, I'ma ask you this shit one more time!" Jude screamed. "Where the fuckin' stash at 'fore I start sprayin' in this bitch?!"

"Man, in the crib, man! Damn!"

"Nah, fuck that! You gon' take me to this shit bruh!"

Jude roughly snatched Kevin off the ground and pushed him into the screen door. "Take me to it, mothafucka! Aye, watch these niggas!" Jude ordered Tez.

"Don't worry. I got this shit, cuz!" Tez said.

Jude shoved Kevin into the apartment, forcing him to lead him to his stash.

"Fuck ya'll layin' there looking stupid for?! I said empty ya'll fuckin' pockets!"

The three men on the ground quickly began removing their wallets and jewelry before tossing it onto the ground. Tez quickly grabbed everything and stashed it inside the pouch of his hoodie.

Oh my God! *This shit is not happening*!

Seconds later, Jude and Kevin emerged from the house. Jude had the black duffel bag slung over his shoulder and his gun aimed at Kevin's back. Kevin had his hands behind his head.

"Mothafucka, you better kill me right now!" Kevin yelled. "'Cause if you let me live, I swear I'm coming for that ass!"

"Nigga, get yo' ass on the ground!" Jude roughly shoved him. "Ain't nobody tryin' to hear that bullshit! You musta forgot I'm the nigga with the gun!"

Kevin slowly knelt down onto his knees with his hands still behind his head.

"Man, fuck that shit!" Tez yelled. "I say we body these niggas right here, right now! They done seen yo' face, bruh!"

"Man, fuck these bitch ass niggas!" Jude argued. "I ain't worried about it! Shit, we out!"

Keeping their guns aimed at the four men, Jude and Tez headed back towards the truck making sure not to turn their backs on any of them.

"You should've killed me, nigga!" Kevin yelled after them. "You should've fuckin' killed me."

The minute Jude and Tez hopped into the truck, I peeled out of the driveway.

"Please, God…don't let any of them have seen me," I prayed as I flew up Kinsman Avenue.

Chapter 19

You laid up with a nigga you know nothing about.

Silk's words kept replaying over in my mind as I tossed and turned in bed. I had no idea that Jude was capable of pulling the shit that he did tonight. And I damn sure didn't think he was capable of returning home and climbing back into bed with me as though he hadn't done anything wrong.

Everyone around me was changing drastically. First Tiffany…Now Jude…I just wanted things to be the way they used to but I doubted things would ever go back to the way they used to be.

***

When I awoke the following morning, I noticed Jude was no longer beside me. He wasn't in the house period for that matter. The keys to the truck were gone so I figured he was out running the streets. On the way to the kitchen, Tiffany suddenly decided to return. With her pumps in one hand, she tiptoed barefoot inside not even noticing me.

"You're grown remember? I caught her off guard.

She jumped at the sound of my voice. "Shit, Cameron. You scared me," she laughed. "I didn't wanna wake you." She snorted and wiped her nose. "What you doin' up this early?"

I pointed to her blue pumps in her hand. "The question is what are *you* doing creeping in the house so early? You've been gone all day yesterday? You must've partied pretty hard."

"Yeah I kicked it pretty tough," she said nonchalantly. She was vague with the details so I decided not to hit her with too many questions.

"Guess what?" I said making my way over towards the breakfast counter.

She followed me and took a seat at the bar. "What's up?"

"Jude came home yesterday."

"That's great!" Tiffany beamed.

I sighed out of frustration. "And that's not all," I told her.

"What?"

I paused. "I'm…uh…I'm pregnant." I still couldn't believe it myself. It even sounded weird saying it.

"What?!" Tiffany sounded just as surprised as I felt when I first found out. "How long have you known?" she asked.

I sighed. "For a few days now."

"Well…are you keeping it?" she asked.

"I still don't know," I admitted. "I'm not sure if I'm ready for all this, Tiff."

"Did you tell Jude?"

"Yeah," I answered. "He wants to keep it."

Tiffany scoffed. "Why does that not surprise me? Niggas always want the baby but they're never the one taking care of it. And besides," she added. "How is he going to support you. His bank accounts have been frozen—"

"Last night I saw him rob some guys," I blurted out. I hadn't intended to tell Tiffany but it just slipped out.

"What?!"

I quickly filled her in on everything I had witnessed last night.

"So let me get this straight," Tiffany said. "Jude robbed the guy that killed Pocahontas?" she asked. "Is it just me or is Cleveland too fucking small?" she laughed.

"Tiff, this is serious," I whined.

"Okay. Okay. But look at this way. I mean, obviously Jude is on that 'get money by any means necessary tip'. He's trying to support you and his baby anyway that he can. A lot of niggas wouldn't even be on that."

"I would rather be broke than to lose him," I said.

Tiffany sighed. "But it's not just about you, Cameron. If you plan on having this baby, it's about ya'll child too."

I allowed Tiffany's words to marinate.

Suddenly, Jude entered the house carrying two plastic bags. "Hey, good morning babe," he greeted cheerfully.

"Good morning. Hey babe, this is Tiffany. Tiffany, Jude."

"Nice to meet you," they said in unison.

"Here, I got you some breakfast from Gyro George," he said handing me one of the plastic bags. Inside was a paper food container.

"Thanks baby."

He walked into the bedroom and closed the door behind himself.

"Damn, he is fine," Tiffany whispered, smiling mischievously. "Why haven't you introduced me sooner?" she joked.

"Watch it now," I said pointing my finger at her.

I actually didn't have that much of an appetite. I placed the container of food into the fridge and made my way into the bedroom.

The minute I opened the door, I was met with the unexpected sight of Jude sorting through drugs in his paper container.

"Shit, Cameron!" he quickly closed the container.

"Jude, what the fuck was that?!" I yelled. "Please tell me you're not doing what I think you are!"

Jude placed the container back into the plastic Thank You bag. "Baby, I know what this looks like…"

"Tell me you're not doing this shit, Jude," I said in a pained voice.

"I'm sorry, Cameron. But a nigga gotta do what he gotta do."

"Jude—"

The sudden sound of my "Cashin' Out" ringtone interrupted me. Jude grabbed my cell phone off the nightstand and peered at the caller ID. His expression quickly became one of utter disdain.

"Who the fuck is Marcus, Cameron?" he asked in a calm tone.

My heart sank into the pit of my stomach. *Shit, I should've known this day was coming*! I opened my mouth and quickly closed it. I didn't know what the hell to say.

"I'm giving you a chance to explain," he said. "Who is this cat?"

The phone continued to ring as we stood a few feet away from each other. You could've cut the tension in the air with a knife. "He's no one," I finally said.

My cell phone finally stopped ringing and Jude tossed it onto the bed. "Oh, he's no one huh?" he asked digging into his jeans pocket. He pulled his cell phone out and began scrolling through it. "This doesn't look like *no one* to me," he said, holding the picture up for me to see.

I walked closer to him in order to see the picture clearly—my mouth instantly fell open at the snapshot of me and Marcus dancing with each other at Earth Night Club.

"Ericka sent this picture to me other day. Said she saw you down at Earth Night Clu—"

"Oh my God! Ericka?!" I tossed my hands in the air. "You wanna talk about some shit?! Let's talk about this crazy chick. The bitch has been following me…harassing me! She attacked me a couple weeks ago and beat my truck with a bat—"

"She beat your truck with a bat?" Jude's face clearly indicated that he didn't believe me. Especially since I no longer had proof. "Cam cut the bullshit. What's up with you and this dude? And what type of fuckin' woman got time to be dancing on niggas in the club while her man laid up in the hospital?" he asked. "You know you ain't shit for that, right?"

"There is nothing going on between us," I argued.

"I mean, shit! I'm out here doing what the fuck I gotta do to provide you and this baby and you out here gallivanting with some nigga! Is this mothafuckin' baby even mine, Cameron?!" he asked. "Hell, I'm starting to have doubts."

Jude's words felt like fire searing my skin. Tears pooled in my eyes as I stared at him in resentment. To accuse me and Marcus of messing with each other was one thing, but he had gone as far as to question our child.

"You know how fuckin' embarrassed I felt having my *ex* send me this shit?! Do you know how fuckin' hurt I was? Huh?! God, Cameron! Why do you keep doing this shit?! Am I not enough for your ass or somethin'?!" he yelled. "Damn, a nigga took two bullets for yo' ass!"

Tears slipped from my eyes. "I swear it is nothing going on between us," I cried.

"Well, if it ain't nothing going on between ya'll, why didn't you just tell me about him?"

"There's nothing to tell!"

"All I know is when this baby is born, I want a mothafuckin' paternity test!" Jude said nastily.

"Fuck you!" I screamed.

Jude snorted. "Fuck me? Nah, fuck him…Then again you probably already did that while a nigga was laid up in the hospital."

I didn't say another word as I walked around him and snatched my car keys off the night table and my cell phone off the bed. I couldn't even talk to Jude with him speaking to me like this.

"Cameron? Are you okay?" Tiffany asked as I stormed past her and out the front door.

Chapter 20

Since I was nineteen, none of the hotels in the area would sell me a room. I ended up lucking up with the El Dorado Motel in Garfield Heights and I had to shoot the manager and extra hundred dollars for bending the rules for me.

I had barely been in my motel room five minutes and my cell phone was blowing up with missed calls. I assumed they were from Jude calling to apologize but surprisingly he had not called or texted me once. Instead, Tiffany was calling me like crazy.

Hesitantly, I answered the phone. "What, Tiff?"

"Girl, where are you at? I was worried about you," she said. "Is everything okay?"

I was actually surprised at how genuinely concerned Tiffany seemed. "No. I'm not okay," I answered.

"Where are you at right now?" she asked.

"At the El Dorado Motel on Broadway."

"Girl! Are you crazy?! Staying at a damn motel? I'm on my way." She quickly disconnected the call before I could decline.

I was dozing off to sleep when she finally called me an hour later letting me know she was outside. After opening my door for she looked around the cheap, dirty room and made a face.

"I can't believe you let that man piss you off to the point where you'd want to stay at a damn motel." Tiffany snorted and wiped her nose. "Go home and talk to him," she said.

I plopped down onto the squeaky mattress. "I don't have anything to say to him," I told her. "And it's obvious he ain't got shit to say to me either. He hasn't called or texted me."

"Yet!" Tiffany added. "He may just need a moment to cool down. You know how niggas can be," she said. "Anyway, I'm not about to let you stay cooped up in this dirty ass motel room all day."

I sighed dejectedly. "Tiff, I really don't even feel like being bothered."

"But your birthday is tomorrow!" Tiffany said excitedly.

"Oh my God." I shook my head. "I can't believe I forgot my own birthday."

"And you're sitting up here in this ratchet ass room when we should be out kickin' it," she said. "*Ooohhh*! You know what?! One of my lil' friends is havin' a set at his spot tonight. We should slide through."

I hesitated. "I don't know Tiffany…"

"So you're telling me that you'd rather sit in this funky motel room than to do something fun on the day before your birthday?!"

"Who is this lil' friend? Where do you know him from?" I asked.

Tiffany hesitated to answer my question. "Out and about," she finally said.

"Girl, hell no. The last time we went out together you left me at the club. Remember that?" I reminded her.

"Oh my goodness," Tiffany sighed. "You're still on that? Look, we don't even have to take my car. We can take yours," she offered. "That way I have no way of leaving you. I mean it ain't like we goin' to dance or nothing. It's just a kickback."

I still wasn't feeling the whole idea. "I don't know," I said. "Where is this party?"

"Fleet—"

“Oh, hell no!” I exclaimed. “You must not know shit about that area.”

“Oh my God, Cameron!” Tiffany whined. “Quit being a negative Nancy. We’re gonna have fun. And trust me, you could use it.”

***

Chief Keef’s “Don’t Like” remix was bumping at its maximum volume throughout the house. The pungent aroma of marijuana lingered through the air. People were everywhere drinking, smoking, and chopping it up. I still couldn’t believe this many people could actually fit in this little ass house.

A fuck nigga! That’s that shit I don’t like!

“Where do you know this nigga from?” I shouted in Tiffany’s ear.

“I told you out and about,” she said. “Relax! You’re good!”

I followed Tiffany into the crowded kitchen where she was greeted by a Pharrell look-a-like.

“What’s up, ma! I’m glad you decided to slide through. And you brought ya girl with you.” He nodded his head at me. “That’s what’s up. Aye, I got someth—”

“Let me get my girl situated and then I’ll holla at you,” Tiffany quickly said.

It was apparent that whatever business they had with each other Tiffany didn’t want to discuss around me.

“Aight,” he said before walking off.

Tiffany gently grabbed me by the wrist and led me to the kitchen counter. "Girl, you lookin' all stiff and shit. You want a drink to loosen you up?" she offered.

"Tiffany?" I gave her a knowing look.

"Girl, one measly light drink ain't gon' hurt the damn baby," she argued. "Especially not so early into the pregnancy. Here, I'm gonna make us both a drink," she insisted.

Before I could argue any further, a guy suddenly eased beside me. He wasn't very tall. He was stocky as hell, dark skinned and both his eyebrows connected into one. Unattractive would've been an understatement.

"What's up with you sexy?"

I shrugged nonchalantly. "Chillin'."

"Yo nigga let you out the house tonight?" he smiled. "If you were my girl, I'd have ya ass at home barefoot and pregnant."

I snorted. *Please get the hell away from me*, I thought.

"What's your baby? I'm Lamont." He stuck his hand out for me to shake and I hesitantly shook it.

"Cameron," I said dryly.

Lamont's eyes suddenly got buck. "Aye, yo! You dat bitch, Hypnotic! You dance down at um…Alibi…Naw The Shakedown right?" He took a swig of his Corona.

I rolled my eyes at him. *I knew this was a bad idea coming here*, I told myself.

"Aw shit! We 'bout to get some entertainment poppin' off in this bitch!" he said excitedly.

A few people standing around in the kitchen looked in our direction. My cheeks quickly flushed in embarrassment. "No, I'm not dancing," I told him.

"What? Why not? Shit, I got money." With his free hand, he dug into his jeans pocket and pulled out a knot of money.

"I said I'm not entertaining tonight," I repeated in a stern tone.

He took another swig of his beer. "Well fuck it then. You ain't gotta dance for everybody. How about we go in one of these rooms and you dance for just me?" he smiled.

"I'm not dancing period!" Now I was starting to grow irritated.

"Well how much a nigga gotta pay to smash?"

"Here, Cameron," Tiffany handed me a clear plastic cup half-filled with a blue beverage.

"What the hell is this?" I asked making a face.

"Just something I whipped up," she said modestly. "Drink up. Hey, what's happening?" Tiffany asked Lamont.

He pointed his finger at me. "Man, ya bitch straight trippin'," he said before walking off.

"What the fuck is his problem?" Tiffany asked.

I shrugged before taking a small sip of the drink. It wasn't very strong at all.

"Well, I'm about to go talk to my dude real quick," Tiffany said. "Try to relax and have fun. Okay, birthday girl?"

"I guess," I said dryly.

***

Five minutes had barely elapsed after Tiffany had left me in the kitchen and suddenly I was not feeling so good. My body felt hot and clammy, my stomach was killing me and I was ready to go. Besides the drink Tiffany had made me, I hadn't consumed any other alcoholic beverages.

Sweat dripped from my pores as I made my way through the crowd of people in search of Tiffany.

I made my way over towards a guy who was posted on the wall in the living room drinking a beer. "Hey? Hey!" I tugged on his arm when I finally reached him. "Did you see this…this girl…"—Suddenly, I began suffering from a shortness of breath. "She is about five foot five. She's uh…," I gasped for air. "Very petite…she…uh…she's got micros—"

"Whoa, ma! You good?!"

The guy quickly caught me before I crashed into the floor. My knees felt like Jell-O beneath me. I didn't know what the hell was going on with me. I felt fine all until I had consumed the drink Tiffany had me.

What the fuck was in that drink, I asked myself.

"You straight?" he repeated in a concerned tone. "You good?"

I ignored him as I turned away and went to search for Tiffany. We had drove my truck here and I really didn't want to leave her. Besides, in my condition, I knew there was no way in hell I could drive myself home.

Holding onto the walls for support, I used them to guide me throughout the house. I felt weary and weak. I didn't know what the hell was happening to me but I barely felt conscious.

Where is Tiffany, I asked myself.

"Tiff…" Her name came out as an inaudible whisper. "Tiffany…" I called out a little louder.

My head was spinning and my vision blurred as I made my way down a narrow hallway. There were two rooms on each side of the hallway. The first room on the right was the bathroom. It was empty. The first door on the left hand side was slightly ajar.

I staggered across the hallway as I made my way towards the bedroom.

I tried to call out Tiffany's name again but nothing came out. Sweat poured from my forehead and slipped into my eyes, burning instantly. Gripping the walls, I inched closer towards the door. Peering into the bedroom, I noticed Tiffany walking across the room. She wore nothing but a pair of black lace boy shorts. She didn't see me standing beside the door frame looking in. Tiffany stopped at the dresser and knelt down. Using a rolled up dollar bill, she snorted a neat line of coke off the dresser.

What the fuck is she doing?

"Hurry the fuck up," I suddenly heard a guy say.

Tiffany stood to her feet, wiped the residue off her nose, and then sauntered over to two guys. They both stood at the foot of the queen size bed. Their jeans were down around their ankles as they waited impatiently for Tiffany 'service' them. The next thing I saw shocked the hell out of me!

Tiffany walked over to the guys and dropped to her knees. Taking the Pharrell look-a-like's dick in her mouth, she grabbed his homie's dick in her hand and proceeded to jack it off.

What the fuck is going on!

Tiffany's head bobbed up and down the length of one dick, while she beat the other one, rotating between the two every few seconds.

"I told you this bitch go hard in the paint," the Pharrell look-a-like told his homie.

I couldn't even watch this shit any longer. I slowly turned around…

Chapter 21

The constant sounds of a mattress creaking woke me up…When I finally opened my eyes I was facing the dirty, stained carpet of an unfamiliar bedroom. Loud rap music was playing in the background but it didn't muffle the sound of the bed squeaking.

I was lying on my stomach, practically hanging off the edge of the bed…someone was on top of me…

Tears slipped from my eyes and landed on the dirty carpet when I finally realized what was going on. I quickly tried to get up—the cold steel barrel of a gun instantly connected with the back of my head.

He cocked the hammer. "Don't even think about it, bitch," a familiar voice said.

More tears slipped from my eyes after I realized I had no choice but to allow Lamont to finish his business.

Why is this crazy shit always happening to me, I thought. *I can never catch a fucking break*!

I resumed looking at the dirty carpet trying to imagine myself in a different place during a different time…Suddenly I noticed a cap-less office pen lying on the floor a few inches from the bed.

"Damn, you got some good shit," he groaned as he pumped in and out of me from behind. He removed the gun from the back of my head and placed it on the bed beside him.

Here's my chance!

I slowly reached down, careful not to alert Lamont of my intentions. The last thing I wanted was for him to grab the gun again. I knew he wouldn't hesitate to shoot to me.

"This dick feel good? Huh?" he asked. "Mmm…got damn, girl!"

I reached as far as I could in an attempt to retrieve the pen. My fingers brushed it a little, pushing it a centimeter or so further away from my grasp.

Shit! *Come on*, I coached myself. *Please*!

I stretched my arm muscle as far as it could expand—The minute I grabbed the pen, I reached around and jammed it into Lamont's shoulder blade!

"*Aaahhh*! Fuck!" he screamed in pain. He fell backwards and gripped the end of the pen that wasn't lodged deep inside him. "You fuckin' stabbed me?!" He screamed in shock.

I quickly jumped out the bed. With only a shirt and my panties on, I darted out of the bedroom!

"You fuckin' bitch!" Lamont yelled after me.

People were still dancing and partying, completely oblivious to what was going on in the bedroom…or maybe they just didn't care. I shoved people out my way as I made my way to the front of the house. I felt someone running after me, but I was too scared to turn and look!

When I finally made it outside, I noticed Tiffany standing on the porch smoking a blunt. "Cameron? What the—"

Pow! *Pow*! *Pow*!

"*Aaaaahhhhh*!!"

People screamed and ducked at the sudden sound of bullets tearing through the night air!

Tiffany and I ran towards my truck which was parked across the street from the house. People were running in every which direction outside trying to avoid the possibility of becoming a victim.

This motherfucker is crazy!

Pow! *Pow*!

A sharp pain shot through the back of my leg and I fell onto the wet ground, landing right on my stomach! "He shot me!" I screamed in panic. "He shot me!"

With trembling fingers I grabbed my bloody leg. The bullet had only grazed my calf muscle, but my leg still hurt like hell.

"Cam, get up! Come on!" Tiffany screamed. She quickly helped me to my feet. "We gotta get the fuck out of here!"

I looked over my shoulder and noticed Lamont leaning against the door frame with his gun aimed directly at us!

Mustering up what little strength I had left, I ran to the side of the truck and climbed into the passenger seat. Tiffany wasted no time as she hopped into the driver seat and started the truck up.

Pow!

"*Aaahhhhh*!" Tiffany and I screamed in unison after the back window had been shot out.

Tiffany quickly peeled off, barely escaping the chaos. We were *this* close to dying! I was actually shocked and surprised that I was not dead.

Tiffany didn't stop speeding until we had no choice but to stop at a red light—which was a few blocks from the party we had just left.

"Shit," I cursed. My leg was on fire. I couldn't believe that crazy motherfucker had actually shot me! "Why would you bring me to this fuckin' party, Tiffany?" I asked through clenched teeth.

Tiffany's entire body trembled as she turned to face. Tears were running down her cheeks. "I…I didn't know—"

"*Why would you let him do that to me*?!" I screamed. "Where were you?!" The salty taste of I quickly wiped it away but I didn't stop blaming Tiffany for everything that had happened tonight. "This is all your fuckin' fault!" I screamed.

"Cameron, I'm sorry!"

Tears streamed down my cheeks. "How could you let this happen?! You were too busy bein' a nasty lil' bitch that you didn't know or care about what was happening to me!" I was livid. "And that drink, bitch! You gave me that drink!" I didn't know what came over me but I suddenly snapped. "You bitch, I'm so sick of you!" I yelled, punching and hitting Tiffany in every part of her body that I could reach.

"Cameron! Cameron, stop!" Tiffany cried.

"What did you do to my drink, bitch?!" I screamed punching Tiffany repeatedly in the head.

She held her hands up in an attempt to block my blows but the assault didn't cease.

"Cameron, please! Stop!" she screamed. "You're bleeding, Cameron! Stop! You're bleeding! You're bleeding between your legs!"

I suddenly stopped attacking her long enough to notice the small pool of dark red blood forming beneath me. "Oh my God!" I gasped.

"I'm taking you to the hospital, Cameron," Tiffany said quietly as she continued to drive. She didn't bother to wipe away the blood that was now trickling from her busted lip.

"After you do that," I said in tears. "I want you to get your shit…and get the hell out of my house. I never want to see you again."

Tiffany was silent as she drove us to our destination.

***

I had suffered from a miscarriage after falling onto the ground. Words couldn't express how saddened I was by the loss. I didn't even know how I would break the news to Jude. The crazy thing was, after I was informed that I had lost the baby, I realized how accustomed I had grown to becoming a mother. I might've talked that abortion bullshit, but I had no intentions of actually going through with it. Unfortunately, the decision had been made for me.

Tiffany dropped me off at the emergency room and left right after. That was totally fine by me. I didn't want her scandalous ass sticking around. I couldn't stand the sight of her because I didn't know what I was capable of doing to her.

I thought Pocahontas had did me dirty. Tiffany had to have been thrice as bad!

My doctor wanted to keep me overnight for close observation but I refused to stay. After all the shit that had happened today, I just wanted to go home. After nursing my wounded leg and prescribing me medication, I checked myself out and caught the taxi home.

***

As soon as I made it home, I noticed that Tiffany's car was still here! I could've sworn that I deliberately told this bitch to get all her shit and get the fuck up out my house. After walking into the condo, the first thing I noticed was the sound of the shower water running in the master bathroom.

I placed my clutch down on the end table in the foyer and slowly made my way inside my bedroom. My heart beat faster with each step I took. The bathroom's door was slightly ajar.

Slowly but surely, I made my way towards the bathroom—the moment I pushed open the door, my mouth immediately fell open!

Jude was in the shower and Tiffany had just pulled her panties down her legs, preparing to join him. *Oh hell no*!

"What the fuck?!" I screamed.

Jude and Tiffany both turned their head in my direction.

"Baby…" Jude opened the glass shower door and reached for the white towel on the nearby towel rack.

Tiffany's crazy ass had the nerve to smirk at me. That immediately set me off!

Jude stepped out of the shower—I charged full speed at Tiffany's treacherous ass screaming like a madwoman.

We both flew into the glass shower doors, shattering them upon impact.

"Cameron?!" Jude yelled.

I ignored him as I sent a fury of blows to Tiffany's face and head. One right after the other. This bitch was going to pay! She had to feel my pain! I was taking all of my anger and frustration and exerting them into every punch I sent into her.

"Cameron! Get off her, baby!" Jude grabbed my arm and I completely blacked out. Without thinking, I grabbed a nearby shard of glass and sliced his hand.

"Aaahhh! Shit! Fuck!" he yelled jumping back. "What the fuck is wrong with you?!" Blood poured from a deep gash in the center of his palm. "You fuckin' b—mmm! Shit!" He grabbed his hand and stood to his feet. “Damn!” he screamed before punching the wall. He stormed out of the bathroom cursing.

I had just walked in on my best friend about to climb in the shower with my man. I didn’t know what the hell to think. I didn’t know what the hell was going on. I didn’t want to believe Jude would do this to me but he was pretty upset over the whole Marcus thing. Hell, he could have been doing this as a means of payback.

I slowly looked down at Tiffany who was crying and cowering. Her hands were covering her bloodied face.

I slowly climbed off top of her and allowed her punk ass to run out the bathroom.

I took my time standing to my feet and took in the damage caused. The bathroom looked a mess. The shower glass doors were completely shattered. The shower water was still on spraying the walls and floor. Blood streamed the cracks of the tiled bathroom floor.

Suddenly, I heard the front door slam shut. I assumed Jude had just left. Making my way towards Tiffany’s room, I noticed the door was locked.

“Bitch, open the mothafuckin’ door!” I screamed.

There was no response. After pressing my ear against the bedroom door, I heard her sobbing softly inside.

“Don’t cry now, bitch! Open the damn door!” I yelled. “Tell the truth! Is this why ya mama kicked ya ass out?! You’s a grimy bitch, Tiffany!” Tears streamed from my eyes as I cursed her out. “You ain’t shit! You scandalous as fuck!” I yelled. “You’re a dirty bitch, hoe!”

Suddenly, I heard the sounds of footsteps approaching the door. I assumed she might open it for me but she didn’t.

“I’m sorry, Cameron,” she cried. “I’m some of type of friend, right?” she forced a laugh.

I pounded on the bedroom door. "Open the door, Tiffany!"

"I spiked your drink at the party," Tiffany suddenly admitted. "I don't know why I did it," she cried. "Well…I think I do know…you're my best friend, Cameron," she said. "But I hate you," she laughed sadistically. "I fucking hate you…" She suddenly began sobbing softly.

This chick is all over the place, I thought.

"Tiffany, just open the door," I said in a calmer tone.

"You're right, Cameron," she said. "I'm not shit. I just tried to sleep with my best friend's man…and seriously had no motive," she paused. "I don't know what the fuck has happened to me, Cameron."

I pressed my forehead against the door. "It's the drugs, Tiff," I said. "You need help."

"I used to be so sure of myself. So confident," she said. "Now I don't even know who the fuck I am…"

There was suddenly silence on her end of the door. "Tiff, what's going on?" I asked. "Open the door." I grabbed the door knob and began shaking and turning it but the door wouldn't budge.

"I'm sorry for everything I did, Cameron…"

I banged on the door. "Tiffany, open the goddamn door!"

Silence.

"*Tiffany*?!"

I punched and kicked the door in anger. "Open this door!" Without deliberation, I retrieved my cell phone and called 911.

Chapter 22

I sat on the steps of my front door with my face buried in my hands, crying. The paramedics wheeled Tiffany's body on the EMT stretcher towards the back of the ambulance truck. The white sheet that was pulled entirely over her body was drenched with tiny specks of dark red blood.

Tiffany had slit both her wrists using a shard of glass from the broken shower doors. The copious bleeding had ultimately led to cardiac arrest. She was dead by the time the police officers knocked the bedroom door down.

Suddenly, I felt someone slip their arm around my shoulders as I cried. I looked up at Jude and laid my head on his shoulder.

"This is just too much," I said. "Tiffany…she…" My voice trailed off. I couldn't bring myself to say it. "I lost the baby," I finally admitted.

Jude pulled me closer to him and kissed my forehead. "It's gonna be aight, babe. Sometimes we hit speed bumps that we have to get over before we can enjoy the rest of life's journey."

"Are you upset?" I asked wiping my tears away.

"I'm a lil' disappointed, yeah. But everything happens for a reason," he said. "Maybe it wasn't meant for us to have this baby now. We have plenty of time though. You got school to worry about…" His voice trailed off.

I laid my head back on his shoulder.

***

A week had quickly elapsed after Tiffany's funeral. Things were slowly but surely going back to the way they used to be. Jude's court date was scheduled for next week and I couldn't have been any more nervous and on edge. Not to mention fall semester classes would be beginning in a mere few weeks.

Jude 'magically' managed to scrape up twenty-five thousand dollars. I never told him that I had followed him the night he had robbed Kevin. Nor did I mention the dope I had caught him with. However, I knew he had given it to Tez to distribute. Jude wasn't about that life and he knew it.

Unfortunately, twenty-five G's could only go so far. The mortgage was paid off for the remainder of the year but I didn't know if Jude would get convicted or not. And if he did, I didn't know how many years he would get in jail.

That stripping shit was dead. I already decided that when school started back I would not be end up juggling classes and dancing. I had one two left and I didn't want to end up struggling to finish. Especially since I had come so far.

Finally taking girl, Tiffany's advice I had planned on working a regular job to support myself. It was time to start going about things the right way.

Standing in the doorway of the master bathroom, I watched as Jude tied up his mid-length dreadlocks before slowly undressing. I couldn't help but admire his chiseled body.

"You just gone stand there?" he asked with a mischievous smile. "Or are you going to join me?"

A smirk played in the corner of my lips as I lingered in the doorway of the bathroom. He shrugged nonchalantly before sliding the shower door open and climbing in.

Without a word, I walked over towards the bathroom's his and hers vanity and placed the glass of cranberry juice I had been drinking down. After stripping naked, I climbed into the spacious, marble shower behind Jude.

He groaned in pleasure as I multitasked between washing and massaging his upper back. Suddenly, in one swift movement, Jude turned around and pinned me against the marble shower walls. His rigid dick pressed against my inner thigh as his warm breath tickled my neck.

His fingers brushed against my throbbing clit and I nearly lost it. It had been quite some time since Jude and I had last made love with everything going on around us lately. His touch was intoxicating and I couldn't fight the soft moan that escaped through my lips when he slipped two fingers inside.

Jude slowly withdrew his fingers before slicking my clit with my own juices. He didn't say a word as he knelt down onto his knees in the shower. The shower spray's stream of water pelted Jude's back as he lifted my leg over his shoulder. Our gazes never disconnected as he lowered his head into my pussy.

The minute his moist tongue massaged my clit, my knees practically gave out from the pleasure. Pushing his head away, it was apparent that I was silently tapping out before he could even get started.

"Uh uh, bay. Don't run," he ordered before firmly cupping my ass in his hands to hold me in place.

Before I could respond, he quickly returned to the task at hand. His thick lips encased my pearl before he began sucking on it passionately. My right leg trembled as his tongue slipped inside my pussy.

Evidently, Jude was not satisfied with my lack of cooperation. He quickly stood to his feet, stepped out the shower and guided me by the hand to follow him. Not bothering to turn the shower off, he pulled me closer to him.

"I see you can't handle it, huh?" he chuckled.

"Make me handle it," I said before biting my bottom lip.

Without deliberation, Jude lifted me up in his arms and carried me over towards the vanity. He gently placed my wet body down on the counter and spread my legs as far as my flexibility would allow.

I watched in wantonness as he lowered himself to his knees and buried his head between my thighs. I quickly pushed the glass of juice away out of fear that I might knock it off the sink.

Wrapping my legs around Jude's neck, I reclined my body on the sink. After several minutes of feasting between my thighs, he finally stood to his feet before wiping away the moisture on his lips.

"I'm finna handle this shit now," he said.

"Show me," I smiled.

He quickly pulled me to the edge of the sink and positioned himself between my thighs. I gasped upon his entrance as he slowly slid inside me. Right there on the bathroom sink we made passionate love all up until he lifted me up and carried me into the bedroom. Wrapping my legs around his waist, we kissed sensually before he laid me down on the king size platform bed. We made sweet love in bed not bothering to remember to use a condom. And it wasn't until Jude rolled off top of me, that I was actually concerned about that.

"Did you just come in me again, bay?" I asked.

Jude wiped the tiny beads from sweat from his forehead. "My fault babe. It was so good, I couldn't pull out," he simply said.

I knew he did it on purpose. I started to say some shit, but he quickly cut me off by asking if I wanted something to drink. It was his clever way of escaping me cursing him out. He quickly climbed out the bed and headed towards the kitchen.

Tap! *Tap*! *Tap*!

"Baby!" I called out. "Someone's at the door!" I climbed out of bed and pulled on my pink terry cloth robe.

"Baby!" I called out. "Forget it, I'll get it myself," I said heading towards the front door.

The minute I opened the front door I wouldn't have expected to see the person standing on the opposite side of it.

Ericka stood on the last step smiling sweetly with both her hands behind her back.

I folded my arms. "What the fuck do you want," I asked with much attitude.

"Is Jude home?" she asked politely.

Oh hell no. This bitch really *is* bipolar. She was behaving like she hadn't tried to take my head off with a metal bat a few weeks ago.

"What the hell do you want with Ju—"

"Ericka?" Jude walked up beside me. He was fully dressed. "How did you know where I lived?"

"Jude, can we talk?" Ericka asked.

I whipped my head in Jude's direction. If looks could kill, he would've been a dead man.

"Nah, we can't talk, Ericka," he said. "And you really shouldn't be here—"

"Look we have to talk!" She insisted. "I'm tired of this game you're playing! I'm tired of waiting for you. I want things to be the way they used to be between us."

I sucked my teeth and rolled my eyes. "Look, bitch—"

“Cameron,” Jude stepped in and shook his head. “Look, E…I don’t know what’s up with you lately. But ever since you came home from the Air Force—”

“I was never in the Air Force, Jude,” she blurted out.

“What?!” Jude said in shock.

“I’ve been in and out of mental asylums for the last fuckin’ five years! Come on, Jude! You really thought they’d let me join the Air Force with all my mental disorders?” Her tone was no longer sweet and syrupy.

“Oh my God, Jude. Let me whup this crazy bitch’s ass,” I said.

Ericka looked over at me and smirked.

“Look, Ericka,” Jude approached her. “You’re going to have to bounce or else I’m callin’ the cops…”

Suddenly, Ericka snatched her hands from behind her back and sent a bolt of electricity into Jude’s body with the Taser gun she was hiding. Jude dropped onto the ground, his body convulsed uncontrollably.

Without hesitation, I punched the shit out Ericka’s crazy ass. Tiffany wasn’t here to stop me from kicking her ass.

She stumbled backwards and grabbed her bloodied nose. “I’m finna whup yo’ ass, hoe,” I said walking up on her.

She tossed the Taser gun onto the ground and boldly posted up.

Before I could swing again, she snatched me up by my hair and began slinging me around the parking lot area. She was taller than me by five or six inches so she had me beat as far as height and judging from the way she was effortlessly flinging me around she was obviously much stronger than me.

I tussled and wrestled with her, but I had definitely met my match with her tall ass. After slinging me around by my hair for a few more seconds, she tossed me onto the pavement. Before I could stand to my feet, she kicked me in the side.

"*Aaahh*!" I moaned in pain.

"Bitch, you thought you were going to whup my ass?!" she yelled before kicking me again. "Huh?!" She lifted her foot to kick me again, but I quickly grabbed her ankle boot, causing her to stumble and fall to the ground.

Not missing a beat, I climbed on top of her and proceeded to bang her head repeatedly against the pavement.

"Get off!" she screamed.

It was no use. The minute I climbed on top of her it was a wrap. Suddenly, I felt two strong arms grab me and pull me off Ericka's crazy ass. She should've felt fortunate because if it wasn't for the neighbor pulling me off, I probably would have killed her.

"You stupid cunt!" Ericka screamed. "I'm gonna kill you!" she threatened.

Another neighbor grabbed her before she tried to attack me.

In minutes the police had arrived and took statements from everyone. Fortunately, the neighbors saw the whole thing. Ericka was forced into the back of a squad car after Jude and I decided to press harassment and assault charges against her.

Even though her ass had me heated that she had come to my house to start some mess in the broad daylight, I couldn't help but feel sorry for the girl. She was eight kinds of crazy and I didn't know if there was much hope for her.

Ericka's gaze never faltered as she stared at me through the back window of the squad car. Her piercing gray eyes silently threatened me as I watched the car pull out the parking lot.

Chapter 23

One Week Later.

I made my way across the West side Market parking lot. After hitting the automatic door unlock button, I placed the bag of groceries into the back seat. The loaf of bread tumbled out of one the bags and fell onto the ground.

"Shit," I cursed bending down to get it. Once I picked it up, I tossed it into the passenger seat.

"Hey?" I heard a voice say behind me.

I turned on my heel—

Wham!

I only caught a glimpse of the fist that suddenly connected with my skull! I fell against the truck and slowly slid down onto the ground. A blurry figure stood over and stared at me for several seconds…

Suddenly blackness engulfed me…

***

"You sure this is her?" A muffled voice asked.

"Yo, I'm sure. I've been following this hoe for a week straight. This that nigga's bitch, homie."

My eyelids fluttered as I struggled to open my eyes. My head was throbbing like crazy, I was dizzy as hell.

What the fuck is going on, I asked myself.

When I finally opened my eyes, blackness completely surrounded me. It took my brain several seconds to register that I had something covering my head.

I opened my mouth, but muffled sounds came out. Rocking a little bit, I noticed that my arms and legs were bound to the chair I was seated in.

"Well. Well. Well. Looks like this bitch is finally awake," I heard a familiar voice say.

Whatever was shielding my eyes was suddenly snatched off my head. Standing before me was Kevin and one of his homies who'd also been robbed the night I followed Jude.

Kevin tossed his hands in the air the minute he got a good look at me. "This that nigga's bitch?!" he asked surprised. 'Dude, this is the same hoe that smacked my shit and pulled off. And this the same hoe that saw me pop that bitch on Saint Clair a couple months ago," he said in regards to Pocahontas. "The one I told you that robbed me."

"Damn," his homie chuckled. "Small world, huh?"

"Yo, I knew I should've bodied this hoe when I had the chance," Kevin said.

I began cursing and screaming, but all my words came out muffled because of the gag in my mouth.

"What's that, baby girl?" Kevin asked before removing the gag.

"What the hell do you want?!" I screamed.

Kevin chuckled and looked back at his homie. "Aye, man…this bitch got heart," he said. "I dig that." He focused his attention back to me. "Well…since you asked," he dug into his jacket pocket and pulled his cell phone out. "You can start by calling that thieving ass nigga of yours. Tell that bitch ass nigga if he wanna see you again, he needs to brings me fifty stacks! Cash money! Tell that mothafucka we down at the abandoned warehouse on 93rd and Aetna," he explained. "You got that?"

I stared at Kevin in resentment. Without hesitation, I spit right in his face!

For a moment Kevin simply stood there looking at me in disbelief. He slowly wiped my saliva from his face…

Wham!

He slapped me so hard, my head whipped back at the force! My lip immediately split open and I could taste the salty taste of blood in my mouth.

Kevin suddenly grabbed me by my throat. "Bitch, I'm not fuckin' with yo' ass! The fact that you still livin' and breathin' is a mothafuckin' privilege! You hear me?!"

I started gasping for air. "Yes," I forced out.

He hesitantly released his grip. "Now what the fuck is this nigga number?" he asked.

I reluctantly gave Kevin Jude's cell phone number. The last thing I wanted was for him to put two bullets in me much like he had done my girl. I saw firsthand what Kevin was capable of so I knew he wasn't shit to fuck around with.

To my dismay, the phone rang several times before going straight to voicemail. "He's not answering," I said.

Kevin's jaw tensed in frustration. He quickly hung the phone up. "Damn!" shouted.

Suddenly, he kicked the chair I was tied to over causing me to fall backwards! The back of my head instantly collided with the hard cement floor.

"Please!" I cried. "Please let me go!"

Kevin roughly snatched me up by my hair. The chair followed my every move. Once I was seated upright properly in the chair, Kevin pulled a silver Glock from his waist band.

My heart rate instantly sped up at the sight of the gun! Lord, *I don't want to die*!

"Welp! I gave you *and* that nigga a chance," he said. "I can't let you live this time, baby girl." Kevin aimed his gun at me. "I guess that nigga don't love you—"

"Wait! Wait!" I yelled. "Kenny…" I licked my dry lips. "Kenneth Jackson…"

Kevin's eyebrows furrowed in confusion.

"Yo, man pop that bitch! What you waitin' for?" Kevin's homie asked.

"Aye, man. Shut the fuck up," Kevin tossed over his shoulder.

His boy rolled his eyes and shook his head. It was obvious he wanted to hurry up and get this shit over with.

Kevin focused his attention back to me.

"How the hell do you know that name?" he asked.

Tears streamed from my eyes. "That's your father's name, right?" I asked.

Kevin's lips parted as if he wanted to say something.

"He was killed in a car accident twelve years ago?"

Kevin slowly lowered his gun. "Man, how the fuck you know all this shit?"

Mucus trickled from my nose. "Because he's my father too," I cried.

Kevin's arms fell limply at his sides as he stared at me in astonishment.

"Man fuck this bitch and that bullshit she talkin'!" His homie yelled. "I say we pop this hoe and bounce!"

Kevin turned around to face his friend. "Boy, I'm running this shit! Fuck you on, nigga? Ain't nobody doin' shit!"

His homie quickly pulled his gun out of his waist band. "Well, fuck it! I'll murk this bitch myself!"

Everything happened all at once!

His homie aimed the gun at me and squeezed the trigger—

Pow!

Kevin's threw his body in front of mine and took aim at his own friend! The chair I was tied to toppled over again, causing me to smack my head against the concrete for the second time.

Kevin fell beside me and fired two gun shots that landed in his homie's torso!

Pop! *Pop*!

His boy instantly dropped to his knees. His eyes were wide open. The gun dropped beside him and he immediately fell over onto his side, dead to the world.

Kevin grabbed the side of his neck where blood was gushing like a fountain. He dropped the gun beside him and looked over at me.

Tears slipped from my eyes as I cried.

"Urgh!" he groaned in pain as he inched closer to me. Blood dripped from his neck and made a trail on the dirty ground as he crawled over towards me. When he finally reached me, he dug into his jacket's pocket and produced a switchblade.

My eyes immediately shot open at the sight of the sharp blade.

However, he didn't cut or hurt me. Instead, he proceeded to cut the thin robe that was used to tie my arms and legs together.

Once I was finally free, I snatched the gag out of my mouth.

Kevin collapsed onto the ground beside me.

"Kevin?" I turned him over onto his back and placed his head in my lap.

His eyes connected with mine. I was surprised when he smiled. "That nigga was right?" he chuckled. "This is a small ass world."

Tears slipped from my eyes and landed on his face.

"It's going to be alright. I'm going to call for help." I placed my hand against the gunshot wound. Blood poured profusely through my fingers. I knew he wouldn't make it but still I had a little shred of hope.

He may have killed my best friend, kidnapped me and nearly got me killed…but the fact of the matter was he was still my big brother.

He suddenly spit up a mouthful of blood. "I'm…sorry…," he struggled to say.

Tears continued to stream from my eyes. Twelve years later and I was losing the last blood relative I had left.

I closed his eyelids over his glazed over eyes.

Chapter 24

I knew Jude wouldn't answer his cell phone when Kevin asked me too. His boy might have been following me for a week but he obviously didn't do his homework. Jude had been convicted of felony fraud and sentenced to five and a half years in state prison after entering a guilty plea.

I'd be twenty-five by the time he was released and he'd be twenty-nine. I didn't even know if things would ever be the same.

Sitting on top of the closed toilet seat lid in my bathroom, I stared at the positive pregnancy test I had taken less than five minutes ago.

I sighed dejectedly and ran my fingers through my hair as I stared at the dark blue line indicating positive.

Suddenly, my cell phone began ringing on the bathroom counter sink. I blew out air at the sight of the caller ID. I started not to even answer. After all, I didn't even know what to say.

Against my better judgment, I answered on the fifth ring. "Hello?"

"Look, you ain't gotta talk, Cameron" Marcus said. "Just listen…I know you gotta man and everything. I dig that you're faithful and shit but I can't get you out of my head. I'm really feelin' you, Cameron" he admitted. "And when that nigga fuck up, I'ma be right here waitin' on you to hopefully take a chance with me."

CAMERON 3 IS FINALLY AVAILABLE!!

Excerpt from "The Hand You're Dealt (Tales From da 216)

The following morning, the sound of a baton smacking against the bars of Omar's cell doorsinstantly awoke him from a semi-decent slumber. Initially, Omar believed he was at home in his bed, lying beside Laila. He assumed his alarm clock had just gone off and it was now time for work.

"Chow time!" An officer shouted.

To his dismay, he wasn't in the comforts of his own home. Instead, he was waking up to the cold confinement of a prison cell. He listened intently as inmates groaned and complained about being woken up. From the corner of his eye, he watched Charlie shuffle to his feet.

"Come on. Time for breakfast," Charlie mumbled before nudging Omar's shoulder slightly.

Omar quickly pulled the thin white sheet up to his neck and turned onto his side so that his back was facing Charlie. He wasn't in the mood to eat. He didn't want to get used to being there. He had faith that Laila would use the fifty-seven thousand dollars in his savings account to get him a better attorney. He believed he wouldn't be in prison for too much longer.

"Hey, you miss breakfast you don't eat. You ain't in no mothafuckin' hotel where the room service brings you food and shit."

Omar ignored Charlie as he stared at the cream cinder wall.

Charlie sucked his teeth and shook his head. Newbie, he thought.

"Chow time! If you don't eat now, you won't eat period!" the officer reiterated.

A single tear slipped from his right eye and ran down his face as he continued to stare at the wall. This shit was not happening, he kept telling himself.

“Suit yourself,” the officer said before slamming the door shut.

***

Later that day, Omar and Charlie were standing in the courtyard along the basketball court, when Charlie decided to give Omar a brief rundown of all the prison gangs. Of course, all were categorized by ethnicity and each nationality understandably, hung with their own kind. Blacks with the blacks. Whites with the whites. Latinos with the Latinos. Asians with the Asians. And so forth.

“Watch out for some of these guards. Some of ‘em is worse than the damn prisoners,” he told Omar. “So you got any family on the outside? An ole lady? Kids?”

“I gotta girl,” Omar admitted proudly. “She means the world to me too.”

Charlie raised a thick eyebrow in skepticism. “Oh really?” he asked. “You love her that much? You believe she gone hold you down while you in this mothafucka?”

“I know she will,” he eagerly said. “She would never turn her back on me. She ain’t like that.”

Charlie nodded his head as he listened. He had heard the same exact lines on more than one occasion. Men truly believed their women would stick by their sides once they were locked up but the game usually changed up eventually.

“What about you?” Omar asked. “You got any family on the outs?”

“My nineteen year old daughter, Tamara” Charlie said. And for the first time Omar saw him crack a slight smile. “She is all the family I got and all the family I need. I live and breathe every day for that girl, man.”

“She sounds like she’s really special,” Omar said.

“She is,” Charlie agreed. “Worth spending my entire life in this mothafucka for.”

Omar looked over at Charlie in confusion.

Charlie sighed and looked over toward the guards. “About eight years ago me and Tamara’s mother got divorced.” He chuckled. “Truthfully, I was a piece of shit and I knew it was only a matter of time before Renee got fed up with me. I was a stone cold alcoholic. Would drink and gamble all the rent and bill money away.” He shook his head. “Anyway to make a long story short, she kicked my black ass to the curb and found a new man no less than a month after signing the divorce papers. Supposedly, he took care of her…did all the shit I couldn’t do, as she would say.” Charlie’s voice took on a bitter tone. “The day my daughter came to me and told me the mothafucka touched her…I guess…I just lost it, man.” He blinked his tears away. “Stabbed the son of a bitch thirty-seven times,” he admitted. “He stopped breathing after the eighth.”

“Damn,” Omar whispered.

“Needless to say they didn’t think twice about locking my ass up for life.” He managed a weak smile.

“Does your daughter come to vis—”

Omar’s sentence was instantly cut short when a basketball suddenly struck him in his upper back. Stumbling forward a few feet from the impact, he had to catch himself before he tripped and fell.

Turning around slowly, he looked into the eyes of at a tall, muscular white guy with a dragon tattoo on his face. He was known in the prison as Serpent.

His fists were clenched and his intense gaze bore a hole into Omar. "Aye, boy!" his voice was deep and raspy. "Pass me that ball!"

Omar looked over at the basketball laying a few feet away from him. His gaze then connected with Charlie's.

He nodded his head. "Be assertive," he told Omar. It was apparent that Charlie had witnessed situations similar to this one too many times.

Omar looked at the basketball once again then back at Serpent, who was obviously welcoming an altercation. "You want the ball," Omar said. "Get it your damn self."

Serpent chuckled although it was apparent that he was slightly irritated. "That was the wrong answer, nigga!" he yelled.

A few of the black prisoners on the basketball court stopped playing their game and slowly made their way over towards the confrontation. A cocky guy with cornrows stepped forward in an attempt to defend Omar, but Charlie quickly put his arm in front his chest, stopping him in his tracks. In this particular setting, you had to be able to defend yourself if need be.

Serpent cracked his neck bones and knuckles and slowly made his way towards Omar. Omar's heart beat rapidly but still, he stood his ground. After all, what was left of his manhood was all he had left.

Standing toe to toe with Omar, Serpent stared down into his eyes. The entire courtyard stopped what they were doing and approached the altercation. Everyone was anxious to see the action unfold, including the correction officers who continued to stand their ground and watch from afar. They absolutely loved to see the newbies get broken in, and oftentimes they even bet on prison fights as a means of entertainment.

"I'm supposed to be intimidated by you, mothafucka?" Omar asked, not once breaking the intense stare they had locked on each other. Growing up in the hood, Omar had fought plenty of guys to protect himself, some twice the size of the chiseled white man standing before him.

Serpent smiled, showing off a mouthful of rotten teeth from years of chewing tobacco. Suddenly, he slammed his wide forehead into the bridge of Omar's nose, crushing the bone instantly. Omar stumbled backwards and grabbed his broken nose. His tear ducts stung from the powerful blow and it was the worst pain he had ever felt in his entire life. Blood instantly leaked from his nose and seeped into his mouth.

Serpent quickly rushed Omar and delivered a gut-wrenching punch into his lower abdomen.

Omar groaned in pain from the blow and a couple black prisoners stepped up like they wanted to help Omar out, but Charlie however, stopped them.

"Let him fight," Charlie yelled. "Let him fight his own battle!"

A group of "billies" as they were referred to gathered around the fight and cheered their fellow gang member on.

Omar was getting his ass kicked mercilessly and he knew it. If he didn't defend himself now, he knew the vicious beatings would never cease. He would never get any respect and he knew the inmates would never stop trying him.

Serpent was twice his size and it was obvious that he had the upper hand in the fist fight. Before Omar was able to throw a punch, Serpent's fist connected with his jaw. Omar stumbled backwards a few feet before falling to the concrete.

A few of the correction officers huddled together and prepared to place their bet, which of course was on Serpent.

Omar struggled to stand to his feet before spitting out a mouthful of blood onto the concrete. Serpent didn't give him a chance to recuperate before he quickly wrapped his large hands around Omar's throat and snatched him off the ground. His feet dangled in midair at least two inches off the ground as Serpent proceeded to strangle the hell out of Omar.

EXCERPT FROM "SCHEMIN'"

Nikita Brown trained her polished, black semi-automatic pistol towards the guard lying face down on the dirty tiled floor of Key Bank. She wore a pair of gray sweatpants and a black hooded sweatshirt that was two sizes too big for her petite frame. The hood was pulled over her head and shielding her eyes was a pair of black, cheap rectangular sunglasses. Tearing her gaze away from the lone security guard for half a second, she glanced at the digital watch on her wrist that had been timed accordingly.

"One minute!" she yelled.

DeAndre McCall was dressed in a black warm up suit with a fitted cap pulled low over his shoulder length dreadlocks. "Hurry up! Don't do any dumb shit tryin' to be a hero," he warned the teller.

With trembling fingers, the young brown-skinned teller forked over all the money from her drawer. Tears slipped from her eyes as fear shook her senses. She wasn't even supposed to be working today. She had picked up her best friend's shift since her friend was suffering a hangover from the previous night of partying. Maybe Chante James wouldn't be as terrified as she was had she not been the only teller being robbed.

The Key Bank located on 140th and Kinsman Avenue only kept one teller and one security guard during every shift. Knocking over the corner bank in the hood was like taking candy from a baby. The robbery was damn near effortless.

"Big bills first! Come on now! Let's go Chante!" Dre ordered, eyeing the teller's nametag.

"That's time!" Nikki yelled.

Chante barely had enough time to stuff the band of singles into the gray gym bag Dre had tossed her, before he snatched it and darted towards the exit.

Nikki's index finger rested on the trigger of the pistol. "Stay on the ground," she told the security guard. "Don't you dare fuckin' move!" Satisfied that the guard wouldn't move from his position, she turned on her heel and sprinted towards the doors.

Hassan Bashir was stationed right outside in Dre's 2004 black Monte Carlo assuring a clean and quick getaway.

The three friends had been knocking over small banks and convenience stores since high school. In the beginning they were doing such crimes as a desperate means to earn money.

Truthfully, they were too lazy to work and at the youthful ages of twenty-two and twenty-three, Nikki and Dre already had one felony under their belt for a robbery they had been convicted of two years ago. Their punishment may have very well been a slap on the wrist since they were each sentenced to a mere year in federal prison.

Eventually the trio began enjoying the rush of being able to do it and get away with their crimes. The money they earned from the petty robberies was not much, but it afforded them the ability to pay bills and live comfortably—even though they all shacked up together in a single family home located in the hood off 116th and Benham.

Dre tore through the exit door and Nikki was right on his heels as she bolted after him—

Boom!

Nikki felt as if the wind had been knocked out of her as she slammed face first into the door. The impact of the gun shot to her back was so powerful that she uncontrollably stumbled through the exit door and crashed onto the pavement.

Pedestrians instantly stopped in their tracks at the sound of the single gunshot. Several people stationed at the bus stop across the street pointed in Nikki's direction as she lay motionlessly on the ground.

Blood leaked from an open wound that had formed above her eyebrow from where she had hit the pavement. She could taste blood in her mouth from when she had accidentally bitten down on her tongue.

Nikki ran her tongue along the top and bottom row of teeth to ensure that she had not lost any. That should have been the last thing on her mind since she had just been shot, but it was. Her ears rang from the sound of the loud gunshot and for a minute she could not hear anything. Seconds felt like hours as she lay on the ground.

Suddenly, Nikki watched as Dre's Retro VII Air Jordans approached her. In one swift movement, he lifted her off the ground and carried her towards the Monte Carlo parked several feet away. Her ability to hear had quickly returned and the faint sound of sirens were approaching.

Dre quickly but carefully placed Nikki in the backseat and climbed in. A crowd of onlookers pointed in the car's direction and Dre knew he would probably be forced with the tough task of getting rid of his beloved Monte Carlo.

Hassan bore a look of irritation and concern as he glimpsed at the side view mirror. The security guard from Key Bank stood outside in front of the bank with his gun hanging loosely by his side.

"What the fuck happened?!" Hassan yelled, rapidly pulling off and burning rubber in the process. "Is Nikki okay?! What happened?!"

"Man, she's fine, aight!" Dre responded in irritation. His main focus was making sure neither of them got caught.

Nikki tried to sit up in the backseat but her body was growing sorer by the second.

"Here let me help you," Dre said in a soothing voice. No matter how crazy a situation ever got, he never resorted to panicking. He figured that you lost focus whenever you began to panic and for that he always remained cool, calm and collected.

Dre assisted Nikki in removing the baggy sweatshirt. Underneath was a police style bulletproof vest.

"You're good," Dre breathed a sigh of a relief. "You're alright, baby. You did good," he said pulling her towards him. His warm, moist tongue slid into her mouth as they indulged in a passion-filled kiss. "You took that bullet like a mothafuckin' G," he joked.

Nikki flashed an innocent smile. "I did?" she asked. "Doesn't feel like I did."

On countless occasions, Dre had taken Nikki to the open field, teaching her how to shoot and even preparing her for taking a bullet. Of course the experience was totally different when she took an expected bullet from Dre's gun. The outcome was all but pleasant but at least she had an idea of how it felt to be shot.

"You good Nikki?" Hassan asked again, wanting to hear it from her instead of her boyfriend.

Nikki sat up in the back seat. "I'm good Hassan."

Hassan nodded his head in satisfaction and floored the pedal. Luckily they weren't being pursued but the sooner they got home, the better.

***

Dre sat shirtless at the wooden kitchen table. Full sleeves and upper chest tattoos adorned his caramel colored skin. Spelled across four digits on each hand with a single letter was the words THUG LIFE. A single star was tattooed beside his left eye.

He stood at six feet two inches tall and weighed a solid two hundred and twenty pounds. Sifting through his weed, removing the stems and seeds, he didn't notice when Hassan entered the small kitchen.

"Aye bruh? Can I holla at you real quick?" Hassan took a seat across from his friend. He looked a lot less intimidating than Dre. He stood at five foot eleven inches and was rather slim in frame. His skin tone and short curly hair hinted his mixed heritage—his mother was African American and his father was Arabic.

Dre moved his dreadlocks from blocking his view as he looked up. "What's good?" he asked.

"Man, I just got done dividing the money up," he informed Dre. "We each got less than a seventeen hundred dollar cut."

"That sounds about right," Dre said nonchalantly as he continued to break the weed down.

Hassan grimaced. "You do realize we just risked our fuckin' lives for five thousand dollars?"

Dre didn't look up when he responded, "Don't we risk our lives every time we do this shit?"

Hassan didn't miss a beat. "Fa' sho', but Nikki ain't ever been shot." Hassan silently chastised himself for specifically saying her name. Instead he meant to say 'neither of them had ever been shot'. He wasn't thinking clearly, but then again he never was when thinking about Nikita.

Her safety had been put in jeopardy for a measly five grand and Dre didn't seem the least bit concerned. Instead he was happy with the fact that they had gotten away with another successful robbery. Hell, he was probably sitting here planning out their next scheme.

Dre finally looked up to meet his best friend's intense gaze. "My nigga, we take risks every minute we step through the doors. You already know how this shit works—"

"Yeah, but it was for five grand," Hassan argued. Truthfully his quarrel wasn't with the sum of money they had earned. It was about Nikki being hurt.

"I said we should've hit up the safe, but what did you say?" Dre asked. "You said that'd be too big of a risk and that it'd take up too much time."

"Dre, it ain't about the fuckin' money," Hassan argued. "It's about Nik—"

"Aye, man, let me worry about my woman and you just worry about yaself. You feel me?"

Hassan was slightly taken back by Dre's reaction. As a matter of fact, he was borderline offended. Standing to his feet, his expression showed his obvious frustration, but Dre was too busy picking the seeds out of his weed to notice.

"Aight then," Hassan said in a defeated tone. Without another word, he exited the kitchen.

***

Hassan approached Nikki and Dre's bedroom. The door was slightly ajar. Peering into the bedroom, he quietly watched as Nikki struggled to remove the police style bullet proof vest. Her face was contorted in pain as she sat on the edge of the bed.

Damn, she was so fucking beautiful to Hassan. Always had been since the first time he laid eyes upon her seven years ago. Shamefully, he was too afraid to speak up for what he wanted and by the time he finally did gather up enough courage, Dre had beaten him to the task.

Standing outside her bedroom door, he admired Nikki from a distance. She was flawless as far as her physical attributes. Standing at a mere five foot two and one hundred thirty-five pounds, her curvaceous figure had just the right amount of "assets." Her butterscotch colored skin was smooth and blemish free.

Nikki's eyes were her most attractive feature in Hassan's opinion. She had these sexy slanted hazel eyes that always seemed to unintentionally flirt with Hassan whenever she looked at him.

Snapping himself from his own provocative thoughts, he softly rapped on her bedroom door. Nikki quickly looked up noticing Hassan standing in her doorway.

"You alright? You need help?" he asked in a concerned tone.

Before Nikki could fix her mouth up to decline his offer, Hassan was already assisting her with the damn near impossible task of removing the bullet proof vest. She wore a fitted white beater underneath, and when then the vest was finally off, Hassan was met with an unsightly purplish bruise on her upper back from where she had been shot.

"I got it from here, Hassan," Nikki spoke up.

Hassan was practically in a trance as he eyed her soft flesh. He was lightweight tempted to kiss the ugly bruise on her back. He would've gladly taken the bullet in her place. The last thing he wanted was for her to ever get hurt.

"Hassan, I said I got it from here," Nikki repeated in a stern tone, snapping Hassan back to reality.

There was an uncomfortable silence between the two, before Hassan finally responded. Standing to his feet, he said, "My bad about what happened. I told Dre you should've dr—"

"Hassan," Nikki cut him off. "I'm fine," she smiled. "Really."

Also by the Author:

My Brother's Keeper

Nobody's Perfect Angel

Femme Fatale: Passion Comes with a Price

Love's Triangle

No Good Spouses

Ghetto Pocahontas

Schemin'

Still Schemin'

Ghetto Pocahontas

Ebony and Ivory

Tales from da 216

About the Author:

A little bit about me, I am fairly new to the world of self-publishing. However, I have been writing short stories and poetry since I was in elementary school. I write urban fiction as well as romance, but I try to dabble in every type of genre. I like to try my hand at writing different things to expand my creativity. I currently live in Cleveland, Ohio. I have no children, and when I'm not writing or networking, I'm usually scrolling through Netflix (lol). If you have any questions for me or would like to get to know me better, please don't hesitate to ask. I definitely look forward to making new friends as well as gaining new readers.

44838834R00112

Made in the USA
Lexington, KY
13 September 2015